handwringers

Copyright @ 2021 Sarah Mintz

All rights reserved. No part of this publication may be reproduced, stored in a retrieval system or transmitted, in any form or by any means without the prior written permission of the publisher or by licensed agreement with Access: The Canadian Copyright Licensing Agency (contact accesscopyright.ca).

Editor: Michael Trussler
Cover art: Sarah Mintz
Illustrations: Sarah Mintz
Book and cover design: Tania Wolk, Third Wolf Studio
Printed and bound in Canada at Friesens, Altona, MB

The publisher gratefully acknowledges the support of Creative Saskatchewan, the Canada Council for the Arts and SK Arts.

Library and Archives Canada Cataloguing in Publication

Title: Handwringers / Sarah Mintz.
Names: Mintz, Sarah, author.
Identifiers: Canadiana (print) 20210154756 | Canadiana (ebook) 20210154780 |
ISBN 9781989274477 (softcover) | ISBN 9781989274484 (PDF)
Classification: LCC PS8626.I699 H36 2021 | DDC C813/.6-dc23

radiant press

Box 33128 Cathedral PO
Regina, SK S4T 7X2
info@radiantpress.ca
www.radiantpress.ca

For Steven Mintzberg

handwringers

SARAH MINTZ

Contents

A Car Called Vera 1
Skinning the Cat 3
Whatever Larry's Looking For; It's all in the beef, hot gods an money men—god schlock and sellin' dogs 5
About Dinner; Self Similar 7
"Let's Go" 8
Old Soul 9
imagine wisdom as wrinkled and wrinkles as decay 10
the god of feral children 11
Always Being, Then and After 12
Colour Can't See 14
Sick Dance 16
Street Trash 19
Karen't 21
Camp Cheakamus 22
Little Wisdom I 24
the Loose Light of a Pale Wooden Moon 26
Reveal Yourself 28
COMMON FOLK 30
Sponsored Content 32
Find the Bottom 34
A Vote for the Vulgar Nightclub Clown 38
Horton Hears a Nu 41
RUNNETH OVER 42
Bunny 45
what you know you know 48
WHO ATE WHO 49
CAW! CAW! CAW! CAW! CAW! 50
TREES AND BABES 52
Tell Me What You See! 53
equals 54
parts of the world 55
Kina Hora 58
Schlemiel! Schlimazel! 59
Disgrace as their Portion 61
Nothing Mattress 64
The Process 66
for how long did the subject watch the bloody finger 71

ah shanda far di goyim 72
Maury the Mensch 74
Eulogy for the Man with the Trumpet 77
a timeless shrug 82
Krumholtz & Me (a jellyfish) 83
L'Shana Tova, I Guess 84
TV חי 85
For a Song 86
"Give it to me. I'll do it." 90
Luftmentschen Living in Cloudy Places, Undoing Things 91
Joke's on You 93
eyelids askance; knows best 97
Please Don't Eat That 98
PIG MEAT 101
Lizard People 102
Crowded Rooms 107
Who's There 109
Strangers in the Vent 110
plain as the nose 112
CLAY DATE 115
till the end 117
INVITATIONS 118
Heart to Heart 119
PROVERBIAL 121
Alice Through the Crowd 123
the Door on Your Way Out 125
Be Fruitful 127
Better you don't 130
"Technically, it's a chanukkiyah" – Erica Strange 132
"In the End, Man Will Probably Peel his Skin" 134
Love Me 135
Little Wisdom II 138
Ladies and Gentlemen 140
Mrs. Yablunsky 141
Question on the Absent Concept Integral to Identity;
or, The Rise of the NBC Homunculus 144
to whom life happens 146
Notes 147

GEORGE: *(depressed)* I feel like I can't do anything wrong.
JERRY: Nonsense. You do everything wrong.

> Seinfeld,
> "The Millennium"
> Season 8, Episode 20

A Car Called Vera

My grandmother kept a razor in her car when I was a kid. She would shave spots she missed on her legs because she couldn't see in the low light of the bathroom. It never seemed weird or gross but to say it out loud now it does. Her car always seemed beachy and peaceful and faded and crisped by the sun. Somehow the razor fit right in with the beach blankets and beach toys. She doesn't keep a razor in her car anymore. She's got a Vibe now and it doesn't feel open and summery and it doesn't smell like dried seawater or driftwood. It's a zippy little red car that reminds me of her sister because her sister has red hair and always used to drive a red car. I think maybe my grandmother got a red car because she would have thought that she shouldn't because her sister's cars were always red then she would have resisted the idea that she shouldn't and played ignorant if anyone thought to bring it up. Of course no one ever would. But her car doesn't smell like the beach anymore. It smells a bit like a hospital, an industrial hospital. Like the smell of the place they fix wheelchairs. Wherever that is and whatever it smells like. Probably it's because of her variety of canes, walking aids with neat features, and orthopedic shoes. All the things she keeps in her car to prop her up, to let her walk and drive—though everyone wants her to stop—to hold onto freedom. But whether or not we take it away or the encroaching smell of a hospital displaces the smell of the beach, it's fading. Her freedom is fading because her body is dying, her mind is dying, and her time is dying. But she wants it still. I want it too. For me, already noticing that things don't have the same shape that they used to. My face, my body, my feet, harder, more calloused, nails less curved, skin less elastic, all things colluding to one day lay me down. And for her. I want her to keep her accumulated knowledge; I don't want to have to squeeze it out of her in an effort to save memories, memories no one will ever see or know or hear or feel again. I want her to keep them. I want the living embodiment of those memories to keep them and keep her body and keep growing until she's everywhere bigger than everything and we have all her memories still, and maybe—anyway, maybe that is what happens. Maybe the stories that never get told get to be known anyway. No matter how stupid they are.

Skinning the Cat

Sarah laughed. So the story goes. She laughed when God told her that she and her elderly husband would become parents. She laughed and God spat. God spat and Abe cowered. Sarah shrugged and said, "Who am I to argue?" And laughed all the way to the hut and in the hut she swept the floor and hung a mobile of dried gourds from the roof and sat down at the table and started scratching out baby names on a piece of goat hide. And God said *What the fuck*. And Sarah said, "Excuse me?" And God said, *It's mine! My miracle. Call him Isaac, and cut his cock*. And Sarah said, "Whatever you say." And God gave her a squint eye and thought, *Weird tone, weird way to obey*, but she obeyed and she tossed the hide of baby names into the fire and made a raspberry sound with her mouth and God scratched his head and shook it too. So Abe and Sarah made an effort like dragging a dead cat through the desert and trying to prop up the cat and open and close the cat's mouth on the dead mice they found in the sand just so they could call him a mouser, and lo! Sarah got fat. And Abe and Sarah saw her swollen ankles and hugged and held each other and God said, *Don't I get a thank you?* and crossed his arms and Sarah and Abe looked at each other and sighed and then got down on their hands and knees and kissed the floor of the hut and God said, *That's more like it*, and Sarah laughed and Abe laughed and God didn't know if they were laughing with him or at him so he thought it was best if he just laugh too. And Isaac came and they called him Isaac and Sarah let Isaac suck on her withered tit while she beat her maidservant and the maidservant's boy with a broom she kept just for beatings and Abe said, "God, she's beating my bastard!" And God said, *Just don't worry about it. Sarah—I don't know, but I think she's okay.* And Sarah held up the broom and nodded severely and God gave her a hopeful thumbs up. And they cut Isaac's cock and he cried and cried and while they were at it, through the storm of tears that muddied the hut floor, they cut Abe and Abe cried and cried and Sarah laughed and God was once again starting to wonder about Sarah until the moyel came and sucked at their peckers and Isaac laughed and Abe laughed too. And God knew that there were a gracious family full of God and good humor and it was good—though he never understood why Sarah insisted on using air quotes whenever she called her son over, "'Isaac'," she'd say, "Time to say your prayers," she'd tell him with a penetrating eye on the sky. And God could only shake his head and make it rain and think, *Weird. Weird way to obey.*

Whatever Larry's Looking For; It's all in the beef, hot gods an money men—god schlock and sellin' dogs
After a 1990s Hebrew National Hot Dog Commercial

"Hello Larry," says a knowing voice from behind a hot dog cart, "long time no see." The sky is impossibly blue, the same colour as a man in a windbreaker in the sandy background, the same colour as the ocean, the same colour as the side of the hot dog cart, the raised area where people put money. A wide woman in a straw hat drags a small boy with a yellow tube around his waist towards the blue water, blue water like the blue sky. Larry swings his arms high. A white kite hovers overhead. Larry turns, led by his belly, in search of the voice that knows him by name. The voice pinches in towards Larry as Larry faces the hot dog cart. "You know me?" Larry asks and dips his Wayfarers down towards his nose, as the hot dog cart tilts and the voice booms, "LIKE A BOOK LARRY." A scuba diver walks behind Larry stiffly, looking like a plastic doll while a light mid-day beach breeze blows the edge of a red and white striped cabana somewhere in the distance. Larry is confused, he's amused. *Who is this guy anyway* maybe Larry thinks. Larry in a Hawaiian shirt, Larry with a receding hairline and heavy jowls, *Who is this guy who knows me like a book and stands here waiting for me, waiting to sell me a hot dog?* "How about a Hebrew National Hot Dog?" the voice dripping with temptation, dripping and running over—HOT DOG—it's soft when he says it, he lets the heavy book of Larry fade away for a second, HOT DOG. An out of focus hot dog with a stream of yellow mustard obscures Larry for an instant but not the beach sweeper in blue like the sky outside of the red and white cabana. Larry is holding the hot dog. "Take credit card?" he asks, no longer concerned with the vendor who knows his name, ready to ignore the jokes the vendor makes: "I take credit for everything," the vendor quips to the who beyond. "This is some of my best work," the voice intones and Larry gets ready for a tour of the grill. "Fresh kosher beef, perfectly seasoned." Larry takes a bite, "It's divine," he either says or thinks, the quality obscures the intention. "Thank you," the vendor says while a woman in a black bathing suit stands with her legs spread apart in the sand in the sun behind Larry, in front of the beach sweeper. "Take one over to your wife," the vendor insists. "My wife?" Larry asks and bends toward his hot dog then turns on his stomach to look at the beautiful girl in the black bathing suit. "I wish," he laughs to the vendor. "Trust me on this Larry," the vendor says conspiratorially as Larry runs towards the beach and a higher voice from outside the beach, outside the hot dog stand, truly from beyond says smugly with a slightly nasal tone, "Hebrew National, because we answer to a higher authority." The cart disappears in a flash of white light and Larry, mouth full of kosher beef, is heard to mumble as he runs towards the woman in the black bathing suit, "I have a hot dog and it's for you." So go get 'em Larry; who's on your side.

About Dinner; Self Similar

The baby was 19 days overdue. After 26 hours of labor she appeared, near dead. She was rushed away and stored in an incubator; her mother Mitzi was drugged and left to sleep. In Mitzi's drug-induced dream, doctors and nurses sat around a card table eating a turkey dinner. Slowly creeping in her hospital gown towards the front of the room, to the front of the card table, knowing and unknowing as in a dream, she woke up and screamed, "BRING ME MY TURKEY." The lips on her large mouth tensed outwards, her neck strained and her nostrils flared, eyes violent and voice harsh and breathy, "BRING ME MY TURKEY." They wheeled in the incubator; Leah could be seen through the window.

I was born three weeks late with the umbilical cord wrapped around my neck. Like a noose. Leah wrote in the "About Me" section of her OKCupid profile. But she'd never had much luck on dating sites.

"Let's Go"

You like the smell of dusk in October in the prairies by the grocery store. It smells like deep fried food from the stadium and crushed leaves in the gutters; and the heat from the setting sun as the final waves are pulled from the pavement settles a hazy fog around poutines and pogo sticks. And everyone filling the parking lot glows bright as the west sun lights up the left side of their creased faces while they walk north towards the crisp conditioned smell of artificial ice. You don't mind your life then and you feel like telling somebody. You mind your life then when you feel like you can't tell anybody. Shout it from the bleachers, "It's not so bad, I don't mind the game, I can get used to it, I've seen it on TV, I don't have a favorite team, but if I had to pick, maybe the Sens," because you love tragedy.

Old Soul

When you're quiet, no one realizes you're an idiot. They say, "She's an old soul." And you don't admit that you don't know what that means either. Either *either*, anymore than when they say, "You're *funny*." And you laugh because you think it's a compliment, though you weren't trying to be funny specifically, you were just trying to tell a story about this time you were seven years old and you were in love with a cartoon character and he lived in the sewer and you wrote him letters, fantastical love letters and desperate pleas for he and the other sewer dwellers, mad scientists, aliens-in-hiding, with access to mutagen ooze, to bring you some so you could mutate completely and shed your little body for a bigger weirder one. You could be with your love then, and live in the sewers in grey and green and gritty romantic decay. And you'd wrap the letters in plastic bags (transparent, so they wouldn't be mistaken for trash) and send them down the drain with a little prayer—and the story as you told it ended with the plastic bag of love floating through the water or brought along by schools of fish as the little fish swam; so you puckered your lips and made a butterfly crawl with your hands to show Joe what you meant by fish.

imagine wisdom as wrinkled and wrinkles as decay

"Do you speak Yiddish Grandma?"
"Yes."
"Oh?" (expectant)
 (silence)

the god of feral children

She kneeled at the foot of her bed, one hand squeezing the other, eyes closed, nightdress buttoned at her neck, the soles of her bare feet wrinkling under her little weight, wisps of blond hair flying from her earnest, desperate face. Her parents stood at the door in bent-head awe of the precious girl giving wholesome thanks to a god they suggested lives everywhere. She, however, prayed not everywhere, not to the trees, not to the great expanse of the mountains at her door, but towards her ceiling, kneeling, at the end of her bed, not like she was taught, but like she had learned somehow. Her mother whispered "shh" to her father and took his hand and led him away from the room so the girl could say her prayers in peace. At the foot of the bed she muttered and urged. She pleaded and whined. She begged and if her parents still stood there, they could have heard the girl whimpering and working herself into a frenzy because, she didn't quite think, but felt, somehow, that the more heart she dumped into this prayer, the more likely god would listen. "Please god, please," she whispered to the buzz of her lamp that droned softly warm and seemed to lend the moment some elusive omniscience. "Please god, make Darren love me and I'll never ask for anything ever again," she swore falsely to the genie god who hummed and buzzed until her parents came and turned off her light and tucked her in under the covers and the silent sound of the lamp made empty the site of true devotion.

Always Being, Then and After

Quickly I should mention that Hannah's mother always wrings her hands in hotel lobbies while the hotel clerk asks, "Mrs. Chadwick, Mrs. Chadwick? Do you have your credit card?" And she stands there with a wide-eyed child-like sweating face holding one hand in the other hand, holding the fingers of one hand with the fingers of the other, her wedding ring biting into her right hand as she twists and pulls, "I'm just waiting for my husband, he went to get my purse, oh I'm sorry, maybe you could help someone else, oh I'm sorry, he'll just be a minute, do you want me to stand to the side, should I just go up to the room? Can we get you the card after? Oh, oh thank god, oh honey!" She turns to her husband who is out of breath, "Honey, you found it! Oh thank you darling, I thought it was lost." And he looks at her incredulous like he knows something but perhaps it's unclear what he thinks he knows, like he had just said, "What did I tell you?" and what he told her she suspects she doesn't want to know. And Mrs. Chadwick agrees with herself to let go of the look he just gave with just a non-look of something like, "*What?*" Though she doesn't have a chance to ignore the look by looking sharply because the clerk asks, "Ma'am? Mrs. Chadwick? Are you ready to check in? We'll just need your credit card," and distracts her from seeing her husband shake his head, and Hannah is glad her mother didn't see her father shake his head, and knows that had her mother seen she might have stuck out her chin and he would have looked at her with his eyelids mostly lowered and his lips smug with straining. And Hannah hardly realized the role that she would play years later when her boyfriend accused her of passive aggression when she sighed affectedly after listening to what she thought was the absurd complaint that she seemed to tune out whenever they spoke of anything except her. "Good lord!" she didn't say but sighed with exasperation and threw her head back silently screeching, "Who gives a flying fuck?" So was she only the short side of a sharp shape that could have been complete had her mother seen her father shake his head at which she stuck out her chin to meet him while he strained his face and Hannah sighed loud enough to make a point about how ridiculous she thought they were? Hannah's sigh could throw the whole thing open and her father would shout, "I'm going for a walk!" And her mother would say spitefully while the clerk waited, while the guests stood captive, "You know what, don't come back!" And Hannah would ask for the room key and go upstairs and watch expensive hotel movies while her mother felt guilty enough to put snacks on the room.

Colour Can't See

I wished for fair skin when I was a child. My mother was brownish, like her father. She called herself "nicotine stained" and claimed she couldn't wear green because it made her look yellow or yellow because it made her look green. I could always see all the pores on her nose and her eyebrow hairs looked wiry against her greasy brown skin. She said that when she was a kid people thought she was an *Indian*. She was small and couldn't say her last name, Miodownik, so she'd say her name was Micmac. And somehow her brown skin and her Micmac and pictures of 1960s *Indians* and *Eskimos* wearing fur coats with big shiny eyes all rolled into one picture of my happy Native mother, who isn't Native. Nor is she Greek nor Mediterranean like she said people said. I guess she's white, I hear we're Polish or Russian or German but I suppose there's not much focus on retaining history in our family. We don't tell stories about the past, we don't pass things down. And there must be mutts like us, holding up their identities with things they thought they heard as children. But whatever we are, I didn't want to be brown. And she didn't want it for me, and somehow, I never got it. I don't know what my father was—his history being more lost and muddled than ours and then distanced by divorce and deadbeatism—Irish or something, though mother speculated with some exoticization that his mother was Native or Jewish because she looked swarthy in pictures. But I came out whitish pink and she called me alabaster and said it with a swoon. And I can wear green and yellow and my dark eyebrows look wiry against my dry pink skin. But I don't look great in orange.

Sick Dance

Strep throat gave Ruthy confidence. She was 12 years old and about to enter grade seven at Langlet when she felt sore and stiff and got the diagnosis. It lasted longer than expected and she missed the first week of school. The tail end of the sickness was non-stop coughing. She was better, the doctor said she was better, but she had this thin tickle in her throat all the time and would cough until her stomach ached. She recovered, outside of the chronic strep she would come down with annually, maybe allergy related, it was speculated, each summer before school started for six straight years of junior high and high school. After which, it lifted, like a weird fog, and she was cured.

But she was a week late starting grade seven and the kids were already getting some kind of back to school *hoopla* together for an interim parent/teacher night in mid-October. It was like a talent show or an effort show and Ruthy glommed on to her grade six friends' dance number. Crystal, Karen, Katrina and her. They danced a little dance choreographed by Katrina, the girl with the most jazz classes under her belt. It was a pathetic number, with the girls flailing their arms and struggling to match their footsteps, but for 12-year-old unprofessionals it was expected—no one was surprised but no one really encouraged them either. Some prepubescent fantasy, budding sexuality, and too many music videos led to crop tops and short shorts each in a bold colour. Ruthy wore red, Crystal green, Karen blue, Katrina yellow. They started practicing in costume in the gym every lunch hour.

    Ruthy had never really felt anything even vaguely sexual, being a sort of dopey late bloomer with a love of building blocks—though she had never developed as a builder and insisted on scattering her room with little cubes she called houses and learned to loathe by the end of the year. Age 12, she was very much a kid and to even wear a crop top hadn't occurred to her as an event. But Katrina, Katrina who danced and had a sophisticated sarcasm that Ruthy couldn't always decipher, she picked the outfits and she engineered the whole image. During lunch hour, dancing to Sir Mix-a-Lot, wearing crop tops while Katrina proxy-flirted for the three other shy silly girls while they played hand-clapping games, the grade seven boys started hanging around. Each lunch hour, more of the boys would show up until a week before *the night* and the gym had become a legitimate hang out. Though Ruthy worried that all these kids were too cool for her, Katrina reveled, and the other girls were moving over, taking cues and learning to be a little coy, a little cruel and still, always game. Ruthy, dopey dummy, was so awkward Katrina might have banned her from the group for failing to pick up on now obvious social cues if not for the *buzz* started by Matt Lefner, which spread around to the rest of the gang and back to insider Katrina who used it as leverage or as a tool to snap Ruthy out of whatever childhood rut she was stuck in. "You know," she told Ruthy slyly, "the boys think you have a *great* body." For Ruthy, it was like learning she had been, maybe, adopted. No such thing had occurred to her. "What do you mean?" she returned suspiciously, confused on what had happened and how it had happened. "Matt said you had a 'six-pack'." Katrina said with little awareness of what it meant—and though she seemed an expert at covering up immaturity and ignorance or anything that made her anything less than what she knew she deserved to be, really, she just didn't care about whatever ignorance she might possess and this was part of her charm. "What's that?" Ruthy said, not at all charming in her ignorance, more desperate, more pleading, with a kind of confusion that inevitably annoyed. "Whatever, he thinks you're hot!" Katrina laughed and tried to joke, not wanting this moment to become anything other than sensational, as usual, she didn't have time for anything outside of titters, and it was fun, she was fun, because of that. Ruthy might be sincere, but she could be tedious. "Oh," she said gravely, though somewhere inside a delicate confidence was born from flattery and outside praise and maybe it is or maybe it isn't really different from confidence earned, but each fades in time without practice, without upkeep, without coughing. The boys just loved Ruthy. It didn't matter that she was awkward as long as she didn't tell anyone. She really got into crop tops. Then she really got into makeup, then hair, and if there were gateways, you could, by gateway logic, say that strep throat was the gateway to drinking. Because she started to drink by the end of grade seven and she started to lose some awkwardness and the look of the little cubes all over her room became so offensive she didn't think to give them to her little brother but instead filled a big green bag. Ruthy was kind of cool and her body became important. Maybe not a direct effect of being flattered once or twice as a 12-year-old, but the cumulative effect of being in the world in full midriff and getting, always, positive feedback. Or even, wearing short shorts or short skirts or high heels and getting looks and love and all kinds of things that make a person feel nice. And she kept it up, this body, with yearly fits of coughing and young metabolism and that was really it. Lucky, it seems, if you value little bodies and men at bus stops buying you Slurpees. And who shouldn't? So it wasn't until she had graduated high school and mysteriously let loose the strep for some other little geek to grab hold of and maybe oddly, make it her own, that she realized that she might have to take a class or something, if she wanted to keep her gut rippled and the prizes coming in.

Street Trash

An injured pigeon flaps a fat body from the middle of the road to the sidewalk beside the bank. Moving along with short, shallow spurts of flight, the bird makes it over the curb and onto the busy walk. People pass. A man with a lower lip like he smokes a pipe stands at the top of the bank stairs surveying the street. He sees the pigeon and resumes his vacant scan. The bird drags its fluttering, discordant wings along the sidewalk like a hurt soldier resigned to suffer but not without the hope inherent to mindless chronic determination. The smooth neck is bent forward and the eyes look down in a kind of anthropomorphic grace. A woman in a purple skirt with a kerchief around her head stops and watches the bird inch erratically along the walk before stepping over the pigeon and moving along. A small mousy girl of about 13, with greasy hair, a dirty face, and an oversized sweater clutches her head and closes her eyes. She stops walking and watches the pigeon helplessly. She runs in the other direction. Two blocks up, she opens the heavy wooden door to the police station.

"I know this probably isn't your job, but there's a bird in front of the bank flapping his arms or his wings or whatever and I thought I should stomp on his head and put him out of his misery or something, I don't know, but I don't have the stomach for it. Anyway, the bird is hurt."

The blonde woman at the desk twists up her face at the word "stomp" and looks to the bald mustachioed man in a bursting button-up shirt, she says, "Should I take this upstairs?"

The man leans back in his chair and shrugs with amused indifference.

"I'll just bring this to the back," she tells him, laughs, and turns away without saying anything to the worried girl standing at the desk, her face shifting from one of shy concern to one of awkward embarrassment. The bald man stares at the wall opposite the both of them.

"I don't really need to follow up on this," the small girl says in a low voice.

"You can go then," he says from beneath his eyelids.

She walks slowly back towards the bank, pulling her hood up over her flat hair. She doesn't see the bird and she wonders if someone has rescued the creature, if someone, barehanded, has picked up the bird and healed its wings or cracked its neck, has done something she couldn't do.

Then she sees it. The bird is on its back and doesn't seem to move. But she won't go close enough to see for sure. To watch the belly move up or down, or watch the eyes flicker or go glassy still. She sits on a bench with a distant view of its pathetic, delicate body and waits to see if the police will come.

Karen't

Let's play capture the flag, Sam said.
I don't know all the rules, Karen whimpered.
Whatever, we don't have to play, Sam sighed and turned away from Karen.
Karen said she wanted to learn, she pleaded slightly and then felt undignified and stood more erect, ignoring Sam's glance towards her.
Let's just go home Karen.
Whatever, Karen said, unable to regain any sort of composure.

Camp Cheakamus

"Tell us a story Julie!"

"Yeah Julie! Tell us a *scary* story!" a small chorus of encouragement arose from the campers.

"Well campers, it's been a beautiful day," Counsellor Julie began. "Don't you just love the length of the day? Like I'm so happy it's long and almost never ends and sometimes sad when it's morning because I had really gotten used to the feel of yesterday. I'm glad life is so long. Though it's almost a quarter done now and it gets scary to think that growing—reaching out towards the sun and sky with hope and unknown potential and like, the grip of gold in your pocket—is done, over, never able to be refreshed, you know? It was fool's gold, it's got no value on the market. One fat chance at building from the bud—then the spring is done, and does that mean the best of me is done? I'm afraid of getting worse, you guys. How can you be afraid of being murdered by the Cheakamus Cove Killer with a fishing line around your neck and a double hook in your eye when the fear of becoming worse and worse and then like a point on the horizon, a zapped dot of worthlessness—when this possibility exists, and occurs, frequently, probably more frequently than murder—certainly more frequently than being garroted in an outhouse with your swimsuit around your ankles—which is just *incredibly* rare—so how can you be afraid of becoming a victim? Bloody death is only an incident. The snap of skin and the spurt of blood is an instant—and it's legend! But the decay of your mind and the dull buried glow of your soul is as sad as a happy old dog. A true heartbreak. The purest feeling of heartbreak. One that involves no one else, no fault of anyone. It is all, completely and unavoidably, your fuck up."

There was a caw, a cacophony of echoing caws, the distant sound of two raccoons fighting far enough away that the campers felt only faintly menaced. One boy sighed and wandered off. Slowly each camper stood up. Some went in pairs, whispering to each other, all the way back to their cabins.

Little Wisdom I

Miranda was sure she'd get shit on her head. She went under the overpass watching the pigeons waddle and walked herself into a railing and winded herself and tipped over and yelped. Landing on her back under the overpass Miranda said "Oof." Then the screech of a car called her to sit up and look into the headlights which stopped before they knocked her but not before they conked her right in the head and back on her back. "Oof," she said again and rose up as an un-desultory woman came crying from her car, "Oh God! Oh my God!! What are you doing? What are you *doing*?? Are you hurt? Please tell me you aren't hurt?!"

"I fell," Miranda thought she said but really she just thought before remembering to open her mouth. "I fell," she said this time in words and let the woman know about what had been only an accident. Cars were honking now and Miranda felt she'd best get out of the way and tried to jump back up on the sidewalk which was higher than she could manage so she hopped against the cement wall with her arms outstretched while the woman from the car watched wondering if this was something that should be stopped. "Do you need help?" she asked Miranda who answered with a question, "What?" She hadn't heard over the honks and the whoosh of traffic under the overpass making an ambient hum louder than she could hear while jumping. "What, *What?*" the driver asked, unsure what Miranda's *what* had wanted, but shook her head then and just repeated, "Do you need help?" So nodding Miranda suggested that the lady get on her knees so Miranda could climb on her back or at least give her a lift with her hands like a step, her fingers interlocked, up the concrete wall and onto the raised sidewalk. At this the driver felt like Miranda had really hurt her mind and so suggested she get in the car and they go to the hospital. Miranda turned to tell the driver that if she really wanted to help she should give her a ride home to start her damned walk over, but instead stood agape while the driver held her hands out in supplication, pigeon shit plastered to her brow.

the Loose Light of a Pale Wooden Moon

It looks like a cut-out of a woman on a writing desk. The desk is white. Like a screen where the white glows. The cut-out is a woman with shoulder length hair, bouncy hair with a flip at the ends. She has a large nose, large eyes and a small square body. From above drops a shoe, another shoe, an entire naked woman. She drops into the two dimensional cut-out and drops too far. She loses her shoes. She is now in a hole in the shape of the cut-out and she is crawling her way out. There is no ladder in the thick amorphous space but she finds she doesn't need one. She's weighed down but can swim a little, like swimming in a dry jelly. She makes her way towards the surface where hazy clothing and parts and pieces have begun to ooze into the jelly. She can grip the dripping parts. The cut-out wears a flat shadow of blue pants and the woman takes hold of a pant leg. She struggles to pull herself up but finds her arms too weak; she sticks a foot in a drooping belt loop and this gives her leverage. She pulls herself up as hard as the gauzy center of the hole will allow but is softly restricted when she finds that there is a ceiling to the figure she has fallen within. The ceiling of the cut-out is convexed outwards about two inches higher than the white, white glowing ground. She squeezes into the slots that are similar to her own thinking that it's only natural that from within this shape she will make her way around either the gauzy underground or the bright white aboveness. Her parts galumph outwards as she sets a foot in the foot hole, her head in the head hole, each arm in each arm hole, and her own similarly square body into that of the cut-out with a sound like a suction. She is filling the space but she can't raise herself up. Not really. She can see a little of what's around her by moving her own eyeballs within the eyeballs of the cut-out, she sees mainly a glowing white board, but she can't stand up out of it and even thinking that she'd like to, she's not sure where she would go if she could go, and realizing she isn't sure where she'd like to go coincides with the realization that she isn't sure where she fell from. All she knows is that she has made herself into the shape of this cut-out and she has made the cut-out a little more like her. What's next is not in her hands.

Reveal Yourself

Echoes of faith, elusive, inconclusive. The first one, her high school boyfriend. He had said when asked by her what he believes—well first he shrugged, and looked like he couldn't have been more bored not by the question but by the existence of the question, it was virtually moot, of course, his body said, his eyes said, "Believe?" All-over exhaustion, and her sitting watching. Her feet dangling in the lake, his pulled out, shaking off the water, "I think someone somewhere did something." She nodded slowly. She would nod slowly thinking of it years later. Later, when she had isolated the phrase in her mind—why? Because he had said something worth saying or because it was him who had said it? Or even— one more option, if there were only one more and not a dozen more, a thousand more—because she had no better answer. And when he who she thought was her true love came along, in a bar, where they do, with a guitar, as they do, and they had been rolling around after that for several months, she still having never heard anything better than what her high school boyfriend had said once, disposably—she asked in the course of a conversation what this love believed. And he, hugging her tightly, like like a father who had seen a good deed done, or like someone patting their dog on the head after the dog had retrieved something worthless, but nonetheless, retrieved it, said, "You don't want to know what I believe," with mysterious gravity, gravity that shuts down inquiry; or else the embrace silenced her; or else she didn't have anything to add. But she was there wound up in him, feeling like he must know something, and maybe one day she would get to know it too. And then, in the laws of her own religion, all she learned were laws. And knowing while resisting, that in the arms of her lovers, all she learned was loss.

COMMON FOLK

I know a girl with a large head who tells only sad stories. She tells me that her stories are not sad because there are other people with worse stories and though this is true, it strikes me as the saddest thing she could say. She says it so that she will either be allowed to tell her sad stories or else to punish herself for having sad stories that aren't as sad as the saddest stories. Either way, it is by far the saddest thing about her. The saddest thing has never been the stories themselves. They are common stories; they are everyday sadnesses. They are moods and feelings and people. They are mothers and fathers trying and failing. They are disappointments and personal disasters. They are death and stories about crime. But never have I found her stories sad, though she tells them often and she tells them sighing. I find her stories dull and this contributes to a sadness that she may yet be unaware of. She may not know that the saddest thing about her is the way she must tell me she shouldn't tell her stories and the paths she walks lined with stories and her among them, setting them up to be told against, perhaps not her better judgement, but a judgement that she has and dismisses as though an inconvenient but devoted servant. She may not know that the second saddest thing about her is walking paths so worn she wears a crevasse in the earth in which she would have to climb out of if she knew she were in at all. I can't even be sure that these are the two saddest things about her, but they pain me nonetheless. Not because I like her so very much, though she has a nice smile, but because her mind is an average mind and when I watch her I see myself harden into something I am yet unaware of being. Though perhaps learning to love her would free my mind from solid ground as I would always be shifting around, watching her dig deeper. And so to preserve the plasticity of my mind and in turn, the bent of my soul, I have decided to marry the girl, in defiance of nature.

Sponsored Content
After an early 90s Corn Pops Commercial

Everyone is wearing brown. The yellow flowers on the table look dry. A teenaged girl with a ponytail and an occupied expression opens the kitchen cupboard while her brother holds a glass of orange juice. "Hey squirt," he says, turning away from his sister, "Meet Lisa. I invited her for breakfast." The gaze of the backgrounded sister flows through her brother and stops on Lisa who shines like an uneducated Seventh-day Adventist meeting the messiah under soft lighting in a grey turtleneck. She holds up her chin proudly. She smiles on the word *breakfast* and the two lovers look into each other's eyes as the brother's voice becomes tender towards Lisa basking in his affection and the ghostly light of Brother Kellogg shines from the left, not streaming in from the shadowed shut vinyl blinds, but from elsewhere, never thought of, never known. Beside Lisa, the sister appears jarringly on the E note of a tuba saying with cold disinterest, "Nice."

Lisa's hand grabs the featured box of Pop's and her crisp consonants sound around the room falsely, "Can I have another bowl Billy?" as the F note displaces her angelic smile.

"Ya sure," says Billy, while his sister's voice-over cuts his doughy agreement, *She's got my Kellogg's Corn Pops!* The mad sister thinks, *Stay calm.* The final Pop falls from the box and Lisa shrugs sweetly to Billy, "Sorry," while the kid sister again appears beside Lisa and the tuba's back and forth from E to F increases in tempo while a violin plays frantically.

Sorry!? Billy's sister thinks and scowls. *You ate all my Pops!* And a dream of Pops popping under the fantasied ramblings of a teenaged girl rises up, *Oh with that taste of sweet popcorn and all you can say Ms. Space Cadet,* as the girl hysterically opens the cupboard then turns to see Lisa flirting with Billy, *with my loser brother for a boyfriend,* the sister digs through the cupboard and the violins reach a chilling height, *is "Sorry!"* She throws her hands up in a desperate rage and turns to the oblivious couple. *What am I gonna do!?* she thinks as a smile appears on her face and the music stops, dead.

"Billy," his sister stands beside him at the table, her eyes bright white as she looks to the left and Lisa scowls lightly and Billy shovels corn into his mouth, "didn't you have Megan over for Corn Pops last week?" Billy's mouth hangs open and he slowly turns to look at his sister whose face is cunning, her eyes having shifted down and towards Lisa who says, "Megan Keller? I'm not hungry," pushing the bowl of reinstated anaphrodisiac away from her to the silent approval of long dead Brother John. Billy stammers and his little sister grabs the bowl.

Outside of the incestuous scene, the image is now one of serene untouched well-ordered breakfast props. Milk, orange juice, toast, the saturnaliac popped sugar corn, and a mysterious little jar of junk. Jam? Butter? Neither suggests appropriate temperance. "Kellogg's Corn Pops is part of this complete breakfast," says a chipper man as the spoiled sister rises, stuffing her mouth, "Ghlotto thlove chlose Popfs."

Find the Bottom

A middle-aged woman sat in a beat-up blue chair in the communal area of the inpatient program at Belleville General watching a red-headed girl across the room laugh erratically to herself. Thinking the girl was insane, the lady in the blue chair didn't ask what was funny. The girl, however, crept over to the bespeckled other and asked what the matter was.

"I don't know—maybe that's why I'm here. Why are you here?" she said with a sigh.

"I don't know either," the girl smiled obsequiously, "maybe that's why I'm laughing."

"You're laughing because you don't know, or because you're here?"

"Don't you know?"

"Know what?"

"The story of the Jews who went to war?"

"Are you Jewish?"

"Or the story of the happy man?"

The old woman shook her head.

"I suppose you don't know anything," the laughing girl said, as if to someone else.

"Okay."

"My grandmother told me this story, I was crying—I was crying a lot—the dog had died—well the dog was hit—I didn't do it—the dog was hit, but it wasn't me, and I was crying and she—"

"I'm sorry—"

"She said that this—she said it took place in the old country—"

"Like Russia or what?"

"I don't know where, the old country. But she told me about these religious men, Jewish men, who were drafted to fight during a war. Maybe they had to cut their curls and take a train to the front—"

"Curls?"

"Yes, with the curls and beards and hats. They had to cut their curls and get on the train and go to war, and while on the train they sang and laughed. A Christian man, an officer, heard them laughing and singing and asked what they laughed and sang about. One man, Yaacov, who had red cheeks, was nearly hoarse from singing and shouting, and in response he asked the officer if he knew the story of the happy man.

The officer asked, 'What happy man?'

Yaacov replied, 'The happy merchant?' The officer didn't know and he looked annoyed, like you, like your face, his face was like yours, with his eyebrows furrowed like he was saying, 'What?' like he was saying 'Why?'"

"So I was thinking."

"Yaacov only laughed. And when he laughed the five other Jews laughed too. The officer didn't like this. He knew the war was serious and no one wanted to be going, but they must, and they should, and they had a duty. So the officer shook his head and told them they were crazy, and went to sit down. The Jews continued to sing and shout and sometimes even stood and danced. The night passed that way and the men arrived and continued on with their military lives of fighting and dying. It was three months before Yaacov would see the officer again and when he did, they were on the ground. There was blood all over and he held the officer in his lap and again he sang. The officer laughed and coughed and said to Yaacov, 'Why are you singing while I'm dying? And tell me now why you sang on the train.' Again Yaacov asked the officer if he had heard of the happy man.

The officer said, 'Tell me.'

Yaacov said, 'There was a merchant and a clerk travelling together with a large chest of gold that belonged to the merchant. While they slept at a run-down inn, they were robbed. When the merchant realized he had been robbed, he laughed and laughed—but the clerk was confused. The clerk thought the merchant had lost his mind but still, they had to go on. While riding through the heavy woods the wheel came off their wagon and they were forced to get out and camp for the night. It was in the very spot that they went to make a fire that they discovered the chest! It was a miracle, nothing had been taken. The merchant wept and the clerk was pleased, but again confused. Upon reaching their destination, the two parted. From here, the merchant's luck continued to wane. He lost his business and his gold and eventually left town. The clerk, however, took his small portion of gold, and thrived; he became a very rich man. Many years later the merchant was begging with a group of beggars outside of the rich clerk's window. The clerk recognized the merchant and gave him a gold piece while he gave all the other beggars' silver. Later, the clerk was out for a walk when he saw a man dancing naked in the town square. Who else could it be but the merchant! The clerk offered to take the merchant home and clothe him and give him something to eat. Then, in his grand house amongst his servants and fish and fruit and silver and gold coins, the clerk told the merchant that he had no family and he would give him half of his fortune to know why he laughed when the chest was stolen and cried when the chest was returned. The merchant said, 'When the chest was stolen it was terrible. Nothing worse could have happened. Just as when this evening the other beggars' stole my gold coin and my clothes while I was in the baths and I was kicked out because the bath keeper closed for the Sabbath, I knew nothing worse could happen. So I laughed and I danced and because everything was taken, even my clothes were taken, I danced naked!'

'This is worse," the officer coughed. "This is worse than being robbed and left to dance naked in the street.'

'But nothing is worse than *this!*' Yaacov said to the officer, 'So that is why we sang and laughed. They had our lives and there could be nothing worse and because there could be nothing worse, we were happy.'"

The woman sang "happy" and smiled wide and her eyes were wild. She looked at the scowling woman in the blue chair wearing thick glasses, fiddling with her long tangled hair.

"So—who took your life?" the old woman asked the young woman.

"What life?" the young woman said and laughed until tears broke from her hot red face.

A Vote for the Vulgar Nightclub Clown

Dr. Spielvogel sat beside me wearing glasses, holding a pen, and pretending to come up with solutions to the jabbering glut: "I keep finding new versions, new takes. I'm overwhelmed," I said. "It feels like an intellectual exercise to try and fit myself into a culture, *my* culture—into a history that's always known its own history. All my experience of *Jewish-ness* is 3rd and 4th hand—and whatever TV-hand is. The only practical experience I have of 4000 year old traditions is looking down while lighting candles and muttering a prayer while kicking a table leg—that and being teased about it by boys who liked me in high school—that and people grinning when they found out, like it was a cute little joke that I'd tell myself not to make but of course it was always the first thing out of my mouth. That and my cousin telling me that he remembers me saying that I don't consider myself Jewish. And the argument we had later on about what I meant by what I don't remember saying. I argued that I meant spiritually, as in, *I'm agnostic*. But the reality is that I didn't understand that it could be cultural and I never knew where to find God anyway. I found *Jewish-ness* a little embarrassing though I wasn't sure why. But I found everything embarrassing so I'm not sure there's much to unpack there. I could tell you," I told him, "the story of coming to see myself as culturally Jewish by a comment made on the CBC about *Curb Your Enthusiasm* and 'Eastern European culture'—as the critic put it—but it wouldn't really be a story, not like a story is a story, it would be something of a confession, like a working memoir and after I said it, I'd have to believe it—I can't trap myself by selling you a worse story than I want my story to be—there's no contribution, no creation—it's spew, the unloading of ill-digested *trayf*—and I just can't find that interesting. I need to map myself onto the good of it and still get the sense of the *what* of it, if the *what* of it could be more than just a neurotic *yada* that capitalizes on the cultural capital of the culture its tugging at the shirttails of—but why— why resist *everything*?" I asked him. "Is it spite? The need to be somebody? You tell me," I answered myself for him, "that's *your* job. I would really love to know how to be any good," I said, "but I just have to make *whatever* with what's in front of me. And appreciate it. Isn't it better to *try* than to *whine*?" I whined to the sleepy psychiatrist who wore a neck pillow like he was on an airplane and wobbled his head under wild white hair, while I sighed and thought of every psychiatrist I'd ever had—of telling them all, telling it all, that I get tired of being myself to myself. More stories about lost little girls. More haggard faces in the mirror. "What is the opposite of me?" I asked and stood up and shouted and demanded that he wake up and look at me and interact with me and not just sit, just sit— ask me about my mother *one more time*, I was about to scream, when he stood up and shook the pillow from his neck like a dumb wet dog and said slowly then quickly like catching the rhythm of his own dream: "A man I guess." Pacing then with a pen in his mouth and his glasses pushed back on his head he continued, "but a slightly effeminate man. A nearly fat man. A nearly fat boring man satisfied with drinking in moderation and watching TV and with everything. A happy fat man. Who goes to work. Who whistles well. Who looks people in the eye and says, 'Hello!' Who carries on a conversation like he wants to be there. People love him. They love his heart but mostly his ease. His whole life as whole as his waistline. He wears a moustache like he means it. He's a civil servant who never tires of sorting through the paperwork of the public. He helps them with permits. He's married. His wife is beautiful and vapid. She is blond and classy and prudish. He married her because she was pretty and simple. That is all. He has never felt love, only obligation. He loves his obligation. Through obligation he is connected to his mother his father his sister his brother his aunts his uncles and his wife and child. A screaming little girl. She screams all day and all night and the fat man bought a nurse for his wife and the peace was kept. The peace in his heart is extended always to the peace of the life around him and so, in spite of the love they never feel, the cool calm peace and obligation and support are enough like love, because what is love, that he is loved in return. He's never been to a church or a synagogue or a mosque. He cannot see the use. A crutch he calls it. A cult he calls it. He was raised without God and he raises without God and he has never deviated from nonbelief, never entertained the question. And of course his wife must follow suit. This was his one requirement outside of her beauty and that she might maintain that beauty as it aged, respectably—that she be godless and raise the child to be civic and secular. While he doesn't scream into the street against the difference of belief, he does vote against it with firm intent and the only hope he maintains about life: that everyone should be as happy with his life as he is. That everyone should accept what is presented and brush their hair and brush their teeth and exercise moderately for health, but not for looks, unless you are a woman because that's different. Of course it is. There's no question that life is different for a woman. It is just life. Of course things happen. He's had a flat tire, to his dismay. But he has an auto club membership. He's had his wallet stolen, but it's simply a matter of cancelling the cards and filling out the paperwork. It's an orderly life. Every problem has a solution. And so what. That's the way he likes it."

And while he waxed over me I thought it'd be really funny if I took up his pillow and wrapped it around my neck and sat in his brown leather chair and put a pen in my mouth so that when he looked at me I could cock my head and say, "Are we just about ready to begin?"

Horton Hears a Nu

In a cupboard above the fridge (a fridge, incidentally, her grand-parents call "the crying Arab" for the sound that it makes when the motor kicks on) alongside a cardboard green top hat covered in clunky plastic four leaf clovers, and a set of cowboy hat salt and pepper shakers, is the only Sabbath menorah Sheila's ever known: a three pronged brass holder with a circular center featuring a woman in profile lighting candles and waving her hands towards her closed eyes. In the center of the small woman's candle holder, a circle suggests another woman who lights candles and waves the heat and prayer towards her face. The implication then, that one might light the candles held in brass and become like a small carved picture—an urn of un-motion replicated by the giants that circumscribe the life that contains infinite miniatures and expanding matryoshki repeating outwards in time—if only for the moment when the candle is lit. The recursive Droste like the pulsing heartbeat of a living history—one that radiates and remains, simultaneously, still.

RUNNETH OVER

Gulp was pregnant before she realized what had happened. And furthermore, by the time the baby arrived he was much too big to be carried around. *Unwieldy*, that's what she called him. Though she wouldn't have told him that but perhaps he knew and perhaps that's the reason he never smiled. He had other talents besides, so that his face was stern was no big deal, ultimately. Well, not to him, but it was to Gulp who was always oppressed not only by the size of him and the weight of him, but by his personality. When he was small, but large, as he always was and would continue to be, she dropped him more frequently than she could admit. She always felt that he was just outside of her grasp, she never had a good grip. It wasn't from his squirming specifically, but that didn't help. It had much more to do with her weak arms and darting eyes. She, trying to stay abreast of the world and the events around them both, held the baby with the kind of absence born of obsessive concern. Her primary focus, as it was, to protect the massive bundle, distracted her from the activity of the bundle itself; always on the lookout, she was, for whatever might be next, the next threat, the next corner, the next bump in the sidewalk. And so she missed, frequently, with her eyes on the carpet or out the window, the corners of rooms and the furniture within. The boy's head was all beaten up, banged and bruised, and she so much regretted his pitiful state that she wept constantly and begged for help but the doctors she visited would only chuckle softly and say that she needn't worry about one bump or two bumps. She was too tight and precise and the doctors could never see the real danger of her. Of course it wasn't their fault; they asked the same questions of her that they would have asked of any wailing lunatic, and she, Gulp, was not that sort of lunatic. Their methods failed her and failed the child and yet, everyone had really done their best. There was one day in which she took the boy to a large city park under a very bright sun. Gulp was blinded by the sky when she tripped on the emerged root of an immense oak tree and nearly, given her momentum at the time, projected the boy bundle, football-like into the park's open space. Instead she caught him after having almost flung him and rolled with him a little ways along the grass. When she looked down, she looked with terror, fearful that her roll had crushed the boy's skull and flattened his round belly and broken his big bones. She saw that he lived and that he was more or less all right, although she had poked him deeply in the left eye during the tumble, or more likely the aborted toss, and the eye was now red and slightly swollen. This time she didn't take him to the doctor, being convinced that they would say what they generally said, which is just that mothers aren't perfect and babies are stronger than they look and nothing is serious and shut up Gulp, shut up. But years later when she would watch him on TV and his left eye would twitch or squint, she would cringe deeply and shrink.

The child's rise to fame had been substantially less momentous than one would expect from anything called a "rise to fame." It was entirely scripted, par for the course, the way the cookie crumbles nowadays, these days, in the days like these. The biggest surprise to Gulp—well, there were several and it might be impossible to weigh them—but the primary surprise was the reemergence of the boy's father, who, looking like an MTV cowboy, appeared one day with a request to take the child for ice cream. Gulp couldn't see why not and rather welcomed the relief from the boy's insistent accusatory and sullen stare. They returned later in the evening having apparently participated in a contest in which if the boy was found to be within the narrow parameters for winning the contest, he would win the contest. The boy sang a country song before a panel of personalities and was found to be something or other. The father then, Georgio no less, insisted on recurring. Gulp, for her part, could not resist the intrigue and was even featured on television once in the wings of the stage with her ex-lover while they hugged, cheered, and pleaded with God for their crook-eyed creation. After that scene on the stage, Gulp's place in the child's life lessened and lessened until she was old and he was older and her exposure to him incremental: her birthday, several holidays, when observed through the television. Although his fame didn't last. The cute way in which he over-enunciated his vowels and gurgled his R's lost favor with a large audience in time, and if it were to be remembered it would have been remembered as a fad. His particularities however, were too particular to be remembered at all. Perhaps in a later age the distinct aspects of his affectations could be parsed and spread, but when the boy performed at the time in which the boy performed, there was little attention to the distinct physicality of his way of winning and much more attention to the overall effect. During the height of his fame when Gulp would watch him and wonder how he could be so much of her and so little, she would sit on the couch he once rolled off of and look into the condemnation he offered in his strangely serious televisual eye. By the time the crowds had tired of the stern-faced crater-headed squinting boy, the father too had vanished and the elder boy and his aging mother sat across from each other over the kitchen table with little to say about how they had come to this. And of course when you don't know where you are it's difficult to know where to go, and so they could only sit there at the kitchen table, elbows and forearms spread over an unnecessarily padded plastic table cloth, looking at each other for a long while, each thinking about the other and each feeling what they were sure was the wrong thing to feel.

Bunny

Lloyd Bunowski always wanted people to call him Bunny. He thought it should be his nickname. It never came up though and he was reluctant to force it. *Maybe one day*, Lloyd thought. He never liked the name Lloyd. It was his father's name and he felt it suited a man like his father, a squeamish layabout with thick glasses and a perpetually unbuttoned plaid shirt. Lloyd saw himself differently. He was tidy, put together. He wore black all the time. He was svelte; his clothes fit. His hair was shaved to his skull. He wore glasses but they weren't thick or square, they were small circles rimmed in clear frames and he felt they were sophisticated. Lloyd was neither young nor old. He hadn't quite started his life but he had, some years since, finished his education. He had no clear passion aside from passion itself. A passion to rot the bones. He longed to be involved, to be absorbed by his life, by his interests, and by a crowd of admirable admirers who would call him Bunny. He would not be self-conscious. He would be distinguished only as much as it would be respectable to be distinguished. Everyone he knew would have some minor distinction, some fitting name. But he had no direction and he was hesitant to take the steps involved in becoming good because these steps might prove incorrect, and his time, he felt, would be wasted. But something must be done. In an attempt to be led by fate, Lloyd followed, for a while, flickers of feelings and first impressions. He set up a small studio in his father's garage. In the corner of the garage there were stacks of magazines and Lloyd flipped through the brittle pages while sitting at his work table. When Lloyd's father, Lloyd, came out to visit, he said to his son, "What's cookin'?" in his jocular way. Lloyd was annoyed, he thought his father didn't fit. He felt suddenly, in the presence of his jittery dad, like a fraud; he noticed the oil cooked into the garage floor, the colourful plastic bins arranged tidily along the walls, and the suffocating warmth of the cement place. But he loved his father and he didn't want to hurt him until he had some replacement. And still, he knew he couldn't be honest. If he were to tell his father he was "searching for inspiration," his father would chuckle nicely and Lloyd would feel smaller and sadder than before. "Just working, Pop," Lloyd said with a deep blasé voice. Lloyd's father couldn't tell if Lloyd was joking or alluding to an important project of which he knew nothing about, so he sighed and told him, "Okay, son." Lloyd himself didn't know if he had been trying to make a joke or not and felt somewhat defensive about both the joke and the seriousness with which he was taking his search for inspiration. He hoped to use his irritable indeterminacy productively.

The little mouths caught Lloyd's eye. He began cutting mouths from the magazine he had been flipping idly through. After an hour, he had many mouths. There were large mouths and very small mouths, smiling toothy mouths, open talking mouths, and a few little lines of pink that seemed, when removed from their faces, hardly like mouths at all. He liked how they looked cut out of the magazines. He liked how the faces in the magazine looked without their features, patterned by other images. He felt encouraged by the scrap he had generated on his work table. Though, by now he had hoped that he would have had a sense of what to do with the mouths. He looked a long while. He arranged them on a blank sheet. The mouths made what he thought was a jigsaw puzzle to which only he knew the desired end shape. Again, he felt encouraged by the process. He glued down the mouths and his hope grew. An artist, a mixed media artist. He could take whatever he saw and make it into whatever he wanted. Whatever his heart held open for him. He thought that his next piece would be a collage of hearts. He was careful with the glue. He was meticulous in his placement. Each time he placed a mouth on the page he became convinced of his own truth, his own reality, of his sure path. But the project was nearing an end. He was running out of space on the page. He was running out of mouths. And when he focused on each small piece, when he glued carefully and placed slowly, he was involved and he was undeniable, but when he looked at what he had made as a whole, he looked as though his father would look and he heard his father's gentle words, "Well, that's all right, son." Lloyd felt in these moments, a full body pinch. He refocused his thoughts. He took more magazines, he cut more mouths. He became lost in the process and generated collage after collage. A mass of mouths. He worked the night away. By morning he was surrounded on all sides by glue-warped paper. Everywhere, there was paper; the disembodied mouths no longer suggested anything to him. The garage smelled of oil and glue and was scattered with supplies. Lloyd's father brought him a cup of coffee. He patted his son on his back and left the coffee on the table. Lloyd reached for the broom.

what you know you know

A red cabbage in a small backyard garden believed he should have a fence. There were whispers of ungulates. The things they did. The red cabbage had always known of the outside threat of the ungulate but as he matured, a frenzy took hold. He spread the word, the thought, the fear. Three cabbages staged a protest. They sent up a ruckus. The carrots went limp. The rutabagas rotted in their plots. Squash flowers shrivelled. The garden fell into disrepair. The caretakers couldn't figure the situation. They lost interest and took up with other hobbies. Woodwork, mainly. When the larvae of the cabbageworm snuck in, several cabbages maintained that a fence would have prevented the blight. While it seemed illogical to some, none had the means to disprove it. That year in the garden, bug-holed cabbages lived short lives, but the watermelon came in strong.

WHO ATE WHO

About the fox with the bushy tail and the pointed nose with a wet tip who runs through the brush and jumps over branches fallen from trees hit by lightning and kills small things with glee. What about him asked the bunny with short white fur and nervous black eyes and nostrils wide open on a small twitching snout. Beware said the large bird from a low branch with a rapacious glance and a very, very sharp beak.

CAW! CAW! CAW! CAW! CAW!

Two birds. Gulls. One flies through very bad weather. He flies through wind and sleet. He is small and easily tossed about. He flies over a tug and is shot upwards by a toot of black smoke. He feels it is always raining. The other bird flies through better weather. It rains but often it is bright and clear. There are windy days but he seems naturally adept at navigating rough gusts. The success of the larger bird compounds. He is well-fed and has many broods. The smaller bird's eyes are clouded by tug smoke. Each bird maintains a positive attitude. The smaller bird, the dirtier bird, the less adept bird, becomes scraggly. He has an odor unlike the other birds. He is slow at catching fish, so one day he stands on the back of a right whale and pecks at the blubbery flesh. The large gull sees this and is appalled. The large gull discusses the behavior with several other gulls; they feel the behavior is beneath them; they feel the small gull is uncouth. The right whale asks the small, dirty gull why he rests there, pecking and swallowing. The small gull says, "Why shouldn't I? It only seems natural." The right whale asks, "What is natural?" The small gull says, "Whatever I do." The large gull pecks the eyes out of the head of the small gull. The small gull spends his remaining days circling the tug for its familiar smell. When he dies of hunger and disease from the infections on his face, he drops heavily onto the deck of the tug. The crew is alarmed by the meaty thud. They toss his body into the sea. One sailor notes that though the bird has just died, he seemed to be rotten already. The right whale thanks the large gull and asks why he did it, why he pecked at the face of the smaller, stranger bird. "I didn't like him," the large gull says. And the right whale understands that what has happened can't be accounted for, not really.

TREES AND BABES

"Ho!" said a hummingbird to a jaguar, "this tree is for building nests, sleeping and eating, not for hanging bloody corpses."

"Not so!" said the cat who'd killed an even-toed grazer and planned to save him for later, "this tree is for hanging beasts I'd like to eat for whenever I'd like to eat them."

Each went away grumbling and knowing the true purpose of trees.

The moral of the story: What rings true for you is only a lineup of toys arranged neatly. "Nicely done," your mother says, and you feel satisfied with your work.

Tell Me What You See!

Look how gross and warty he is! I want to lick him and wart my tongue. I want to eat him and wart my small intestine. Is he full of worms or flies? Which food is better for him to eat? Does he have a tail? It looks wound around his behind like a mammal creature, like a lion—or is that his deformed back foot?? I have seen the conjoined rabbit twin and he is similar enough in foot&tail to draw scientific conclusions about your specimen here. When I last handled an amphibian it was out of necessity: my sister had been screaming and telling me she wouldn't swim next to his slimy body, although I told her, he is a much better swimmer and it would be her privilege. She insisted I remove him and I had no urge to decline until I touched him and he made me shiver. It caused me some shame and so now I don't care if he is homeless or feckless, and since I know him to be both, I feel indifference all of the time.

equals

I would like to marry an ornamental hermit and live in a grassy tump with a round door and earn my keep by staring into space. Though I would have to be an ornamental hermit to be married to one. I don't want to be less interesting than an ornamental hermit. Nor do I want to cook or clean for one or reassure him that people like it when he wanders from the tump to the oak tree and stops to observe a captive fish in the pond. I would need to be a hermit in a small community of hermits who rarely speak or interact with each other but have infrequent, maybe semi-annual, orgies in grassy tumps with round doors—while we all earn our keep by staring into space—or into the pond.

parts of the werld

Mr. Kharms collected scraps of metal from junkyards and alleyways. He picked up pieces coloured by faded paint or rust or the wearing away of use—colours acquired. A chrome bumper mangled in an accident and left in a backyard for thirteen years broke at the crumples, rusted at the bends. Circuit boards whose use he couldn't infer spoke to him like maps of imagined countries. He looked until he was hungry or tired or his eyes ached. He studied the architecture of the non-place. He assembled the pieces in his dining room. The base was a string of flatscreen TVs he'd found in the maintenance room of a burnt-out apartment complex. Several of the sets turned on and shone varying shades of blue. The third television zapped blue and silent black alternately and sporadically. The fourth television didn't turn on but for the red dot on the lower left corner indicating that it had, in fact, turned on. This was Mr. Kharms' favorite set. Atop each television he attached a bicycle chain and chainring which attached on the other side to another chainring. If one pulled the greasy, gritty, or rusty chain it would roll through the chainrings with clumsy pressure. Holding the top chainrings in place as a roof was a partially hollowed out vending machine, lying horizontally, secured by disembodied outlets which clung to the ceiling with oversized hooks of gathered coat hangers. The plugs had been sourced from lamps, computers, Christmas lights, fans, heaters, coffee makers, keyboards, and rock tumblers. The wires of their former dependents were out of shell but mostly intact like eyeballs free from the sockets but not the brain or spinal cord. When the plugs were attached to extended outlets which ran up and down the height of the room, they made a low dull hum that sometimes hissed dangerously. The vending machine held by the plugs, attached to the ceiling, resting tenuously upon the chainrings, was without back or glass but had a frame of metal holding its moving springs and a mass of wires which hung in the middle of the room obscured by the televisions on the floor and the chains cutting haphazardly across. Six of the springs worked when the machine was plugged in and their numbers were called. Mr. Kharms took pride. For his birthday Mr. Kharms invited over his oldest friend. They hadn't seen each other since their school years and while Darius Fassbender made his living and supported a wife and two young children on the income of an Algebra teacher, Mr. Kharms collected scraps and lived by precarious means. "It's good to see you old boy! So, you're still in the same place?" Darius asked. Mr. Kharms said he was still in the same place. Darius asked what the old boy had been up to and poured himself a glass of flat champagne, the fridge being otherwise empty. Mr. Kharms grinned obscenely, the edges of his pink mouth stretched open to reveal his oversized teeth. His eyes glistened. He took a mug of champagne and slammed like a shot the flat bubbly before clanging the ceramic against his aluminium counter top with dramatic aplomb. He motioned for Darius to follow him. They walked from the large empty kitchen through a long dark hallway, the light fixtures showing from the adjacent moonlight only empty sockets. In the dining room Mr. Kharms began pulling at each bicycle chain while eyeballing with giddy fervor Darius Fassbender, who held loosely his glass and cocked his head at the sight of the chaotically filled dining area. Mr. Kharms entered "E23" into the detached number pad threaded loosely through the eaten up metal of an extended chrome plated muffler and hushed Darius as the spring of the vending machine began to eek and turn in rhythm with the flickering of the TV screens. Darius waited for the slow finish of the turning spring and then said to his old friend who stood in blue light wearing newly polished boots and freshly pressed grey slacks, "What does it do?" At which Mr. Kharms scowled deeply and sadly and turned to Darius Fassbender, his eyes wet and his brows cross, "Do?" he said with an ache. "Do," he repeated to the floor. "Mr. Fassbender. It's just a machine."

Kina Hora

Superstition, it seems, I come by honestly. Like I do my best work when I'm not looking. *Pu Pu*. Self-consciousness kills it. Or else, the evil eye. *Pu Pu*. See yourself be yourself. You are the evil eye. *Pu pu*. Knock on wood, unjinx yourself—

Schlemiel! Schlimazel!

I ran out of washer fluid in a snowstorm somewhere between Winnipeg and Toronto. Blind and crying and surrounded by slow-moving trucks, I put on my four way flashers and not my coat when I got out to wash the windshield with snow. "Always have extra washer fluid when driving in winter," my father said when I told him. Which isn't bad advice. I drove another 15km with the flashers on, looking for someplace to spend the night and found a motel filled with wax statues and murals of Spongebob gaping wide-eyed and maybe menacing because he didn't belong there being that big. I got to town late the next day and my father was playing solitaire in the living room and my mother was making star-shaped cookies. They asked me about the drive and I told them about the Sponge and the snow and the space out on the highway. I like it, I told them. And he went back to the game and she asked me about school and when the cookies cooled she brought the icing and the little edible silver beads to the table so we could decorate. She asked and asked and I became so bored of answering I sighed, then we sat quietly. He finished another game, turned the TV on low, and started to pace back and forth between the TV and the half-decorated cookies. I asked him about work but work is always fine, always fine. So maybe I don't know them. Like we lived together so long we have habits we fall into. But what are their lives, I don't know. Maybe it was just getting late and I had driven so far and I was so tired and so we sat quietly, reflectively, and I noticed the menorah was still burning.

"Ma, did you ever go to Hebrew school?" Out of the blue to say out loud I guess, but we all spent so much time in our heads to anyone else our non-sequiturs would seem as such but to us they were normal. We took them at face value. And I appreciate that. There's nothing worse than someone feigning surprise when you upset the routine of the conversation. Oh how shocking is it really when from the wind from the weather I offer you a pickle—

"Yeah but I didn't like going up the stairs where they held class so I cried until my mother let me quit."

"The stairs, *whadyoumean?*"

"I was only a child, I don't remember really. I think they were tall stairs, many tall stairs."

"Anyway, they seemed very tall. And I was so young, I guess I just didn't want to go up. Like you, when you were small and you wouldn't get in the pool for swimming lessons."

"The pool was cold."

"The stairs were tall."

"Well that's funny. Did you learn any Yiddish before you quit?"

"They don't teach Yiddish in Hebrew school."

"Oy. Did you learn any Hebrew?"

"I was very young," she said.

"Well I just learned something in Yiddish, apparently I'm a *schlemiel*."

She laughed and poured food colouring into another batch of icing while talking and jamming the spoon into her mouth. Then smacking her lips, spitting icing and waving the spoon she said, "There's schlemiel and schlimazel. The schlemiel is always dropping things, the schlimazel is always getting things dropped on him. Your grandfather was a real schlimazel. You think you're a schlemiel? Then what am I?"

"You're all blue from the food colouring, your mouth and fingers and everything."

She laughed and ran to the mirror to see herself.

Disgrace as their Portion

Godless Loli Crane chokes back a glass of *Manischewitz* while grinning uncomfortably in Asher and Abi's small stoveless apartment over microwaved rice and soggy-skinned chicken. Abi takes Loli over to a small table to light candles and Loli asks about wearing headscarves. Abi says they are for married women only. "I always wore a lacy one as a kid. I should tell my parents they've been doing it wrong," Loli says and Abi looks at her sympathetically and says too sincerely, "It's okay." Asher and Abi pick up prayer books and Loli asks sheepishly if she should be doing something. Asher hands her a spare and keeps muttering. He and Abi are pacing in separate directions and Loli mimics and picks a page and starts reading the English side. The Hebrew looks beautiful and maybe a bit magical, just the shape of the letters, but the translation is like, "You Should Think of God All the Time. All The Time. Never Not Think Of God." *It's really empty stuff*, she thinks and also wants to know why, if God were writing this or being quoted or referenced, he isn't more involved in some kind of artistic manipulation? *Couldn't God make something so beautiful you would fall before it? Though maybe that's the earth*, she considers, *like the awe from around you. But there's no words in that. Maybe there can't be words in that or it wouldn't be that. But how can the earth be filled with mountains and humans are filled with architecture and God, or is it liturgy, is filled with repetition and torpor?* She looks at the English words and they seem stupid and confused. She stares at the plain white wall and thinks she would like to do something with her heart. *Like something that is the right thing after seeing and feeling the mountains and streams but swaying and rocking and muttering and making up tricks to have lights on Fridays without touching the switch seems insane.* And when what's his name, Asher, said, "I find all this stuff reassuring, all the ritual and knowing what you have to do and when, it makes it easy, you know?" Loli had nodded because she did know, she does know what he means, *like, there's a system and when you obey the system things can get really simple for you. But the rituals of religion seem like a lot of learning with no pay off. Like with study, the pay off is these moments of clarity, whether in writing, reading, discussion—and the promise of more clarity and the compounded clarity of things known fall into a pool of knowledge that mingles together and makes something new, but something that makes sense because you were studying the right things—instead of like this drugged version of thinking where all useless ego knowledge dwells in a dark well and when someone pulls the rope up rises an old wooden bucket of depraved ramblings like stagnant water—when you have ideas that are wrong because the input is wrong, or there is no input. So maybe if you worship and read God a thousand times a day it will be at least better than masturbation and television and headlines on the internet because you won't be thinking about being inside your own gross brain but about serving something at least a little outdoors. Though maybe if you instead study something really beautiful or really sound whatever finds its way to the light from within wherever all the processing happens will be some version of that beauty—depending on what kind of muscle memory you need. And with creating, I mean, you don't need much beyond the basics for muscle memory, but you do probably need some structure or else it's still only your sad shack painted pretty colours and not like a grand public building with ornate archways and carved marble angels.*

Asher stops reading and smiles and sits and pours some wine. He waves his hand in front of Loli who is still standing and staring blankly ahead, nearly drooling all over his prayer book. "Do you know shalom aleichem?" he asks and Loli wakes up.

"*Fiddler?*" she asks. Abi sits down and presses her brows together. Asher nods slowly and starts singing, "Shalom aleichem malachei hash sharet," Abi joins in, "malachei elyon," looking at Loli expectantly, hopefully, while Loli regrets accepting the invitation and starts wondering if God even cares about God anyway and if these rituals have anything to do with God. She isn't sure because she can't speak Hebrew so she nods her head rhythmically and hums in roughly the same pitchy way as they sing and wonders some more—she wonders more than she learns—*is being off-key a measure of devotion?* When they finish Loli says, "I thought you meant the man." And they look at her like they don't know those words but they don't ask her anything about it.

Nothing Mattress

In my early 20s, I worked as a dancer and slept on the floor. I wasn't a good dancer but I thought maybe I had some quality, some charm. I yammered on to the guests and bilked them with youth or something like hypnosis. I started making enough money that I could afford things but I wasn't always sure what I wanted so I wasted money on drink and spent money on drugs and took long cab rides from far-away places and went broke before knowing wealth. And then, in the midst of it all, I thought I'd buy a bed. A bed is a reasonable buy, an adult buy, a responsible buy. I walked into the mattress warehouse wearing all white, like a mattress maybe, and started asking questions. I asked about types of beds and prices of beds and kept getting bored by the answers—then I mentioned something I saw on TV about space mattresses or about astronauts loving this special type of new material now used in the finest mattresses and if the salesman could tell me what I was talking about, I'd buy it. He knew right away, he knew I wanted a memory foam mattress and he wasn't sure about outer space, but it sounded close enough. And we walked past all the rows of bent up laid down affordable mattresses: queen, king, super-single, no waterbeds though, waterbeds aren't respectable, although I had one as a teenager and I thought it was pretty good—I left it in the backyard of a derelict house after skipping out on rent because the place had bugs, and never saw that super-single free-flow waterbed again—anyway we walked all the way to a set of small stairs covered in a plusher-than-berber berber and edged in gold-coloured metal. Climbing the steps, though, I felt like the salesman didn't believe in me, I got the feeling he thought he was wasting his time, like no little girl in a white mini skirt would ever shell out for a mattress up the plusher-than-berber steps. And when he pointed to the memory foam space-age mattress of my TV dreams, he pointed with an indifferent glance around the room, and in that moment I sat on the bed and jumped up and said, "I'll take it!" It didn't shock him but I was ready to play it cool till the end too. Up to the cash, no money down, sure I can afford it, I can afford anything, I'm taking a taxi home. Him I never saw again, outside of fevered dreams tossing, sweating on a sinking mattress, holding me, hot, drowning, drowning me. I slept on the floor the second night. I sold it to Ginger the third night for a quick $700, a fraction of what I had paid, but told myself: no money down, no matter.

The Process

Jolene worked in theatre. She was a playwright but she took part in the whole process. She helped with casting and set design and because it was a small theater scene, everybody sort of did everything. She wrote complicated relationship dramas about characters with non-specific problems meant to manifest in physical desperation. She was always so particular about casting. She was always looking for things like mood and tone and whether or not something was *working*. This was her famous line, "It just isn't *werking*," she would say with a strange flex of her face. There might have been an entire terminology for it, I can't say, I don't know the theatre and I only knew her socially. We met at a party. Some vernissage over wine and cheese. She was easy to talk to, but again, like that which she made emerge in scenes and sought always in her actors, suffused with an effective non-specificity. Which annoyed me and whatever I am at this point, someone very concerned with the shape of ideas and the meaning of words, someone ineffectively seeking an elusive specificity. She would float through conversations though with her head held up and the underside of her chin always showing. She was always *pursuing* an idea. I was jealous, of course, but I thought I could learn something by being near her, that whatever she pulled at for ideas would crack open and pour down and all around her. I struggle for ideas and get hung up on words—though I love words; I love the way they look together and what they build from where they stand in relation to each other at a remove from both what they mean and what they are: a world of shapes arranged into the shape of a world. And Jolene did that too, she did, but there was so much wordless space in her writing and direction. So many ellipses, which I suppose aren't so different from words, they, the dots, also point. But it was really how she arranged her arrows that made her plays successful. I didn't like them myself, having a hard time with the stage and all its staginess and its embarrassing projection, but I knew, I think I knew, that when I watched say, that one play she wrote about the wood nymph chafed by a shiftless satyr in a damp basement suite played by a neatly dishevelled red-headed woman seeking absence beyond the junk that filled the room, and was, in a weird way, inside the space carved out by Jolene—I mean, I knew that she had really made something. And me, it always comes back to me for me, I can never be sure that anything is really there in my own work, that I have succeeded in making a world of abstracts seem concrete.

But anyway, that first night that I met Jolene she told me about the stalking part of her process. She called it stealing. She said she "steals impressions" and "steals the lives [she] gives them." She would follow people around. And it seemed to me, as I watched her breakable little face, her harmless wispy little hands, like something she might be good at. She, who never seemed entirely present, could probably get away with a kind of ethereal spying. Like she wouldn't have to hide behind a tree or slink into a doorway or alley, she would just watch her target with that absence that characterized her interactions with everything, and they wouldn't see her at all, if she didn't want them to. Well that's what I thought and I admired the thought, though what she told me was entirely different. She told me about this time she was wandering through a department store—and I like to imagine that she had no impure impulse, like she wouldn't be so base as to buy something cheaply made and overpriced, but she didn't say why she was there. She did however, tell me that while she was there she noticed, near a sales rack, a blond woman. "She was big, you know? Like too bulky for the clothes she had on, not that she shouldn't, I wouldn't say what a person should wear, I would never, unless of course I dressed them for my play, but in life, no, no, no, no, no! And so it wasn't wrong, her choice, I mean, but there was *something*. She was *off*. It's hard for me to say how, in what way, but it seemed like, not that she shouldn't be wearing those clothes, but that she *wouldn't* be wearing those clothes. And maybe it was something about her makeup too, maybe she had too much makeup on—but as I say that, I know it isn't that. It wasn't that! It wasn't like the amount of makeup it's like she wore someone else's makeup. Ay! That's it. She wore someone else's makeup? Anyway, she seemed *off*, you know? So I had to follow her. I followed her for maybe 45 minutes. I watched her pick up items and they seemed at random, she wasn't, it seemed, shopping for sweaters or shoes or makeup or even men's boxer shorts, but she inspected all those things as though she was trying to make it seem as though she shopped for these things. It was very odd I thought. And then, from a corner somewhere, emerged a man and a child, hers, I supposed. Or at least what appeared was a man in a tacky leather coat who kissed her cheek stiffly and took her elbow, along with an awkward teenager who greeted the blond woman with some formal affection. Like if they were Russian royalty or, I don't know, if they were showing off for me. But I didn't think they could see me. I don't hide, but I was careless you know? Not careless like careless, careless like without a care, like without weight. I was barely there, sure. So anyway they were all *off*... the whole lot of them. Though like I said, it was very hard to pinpoint really what was wrong with them. So I followed them until, well, until nothing happened. I had to say, 'Oh this is enough.' Like my scheme or my plan wasn't working out. Nothing happened. And I thought, 'Okay they are nobody. I am wrong.' And so I started to leave the store. As I left though, I felt a shadow swell up behind me, and then I saw that it was the man in leather. The husband. He took my elbow in his hand and I was alarmed, but intrigued, you know? Here's where I find out what is really happening. I'm the spy, so let's have it, out with it. And I say, like we're partners or something, 'So like, what's happening?' Like what's the dirt, what's the skinny, you know? And he says this, he says, 'You tell me.' And then I notice that the whole family is standing behind him with their arms crossed, looking at me! I saw and it was clear that they weren't related. Well, I'll tell you, he told me, they were police officers. They weren't related, and the girl, she wasn't a child, just small, young. I didn't know what they wanted and they didn't know what I wanted. I suppose they were undercover, they weren't clear, they never spelled it out, but they thought I knew something about it because I had been following them. I told them, 'Hey, you just looked so strange.' And we laughed at that bit, you know? Because it was only a misunderstanding. So weird don't you think?"

"I do think," I told her and I laughed. Jolene was charming and had, as her plays had, some dreamy wordless insight. "Did you tell them you were in theater?"

"No I mean, why would I? What difference would it make? We only laughed a little, you know? I spooked the police! I policed the police! It was funny, they weren't even bad, though I don't know what their purpose was, no, I don't know that. Maybe, they must have thought, I was somebody though, like I had my own mission. Well, until I told them that they just caught my eye. They must have been thinking, 'Ooo this spy, we've got her now!'"

"But, you did have your own mission. And it could have helped them," I laughed, "if that's what you wanted."

"How?" Jolene asked (cutely).

"Well, you know how to spot a bad actor."

She laughed a single shrill note and turned to me, "Yes! They weren't convincing shoppers."

"You know what isn't real."

She said slowly, unsure if she was ready to agree with me, "I know... what *isn't*... real." And then she spoke more quickly, "I know what isn't real!" And she had me laughing, that she could see so much and make so much and then miss so much.

"Maybe," I put to Jolene, "you know what isn't real because you make the unreal real? So what is that? It must take an eye that knows what isn't."

"Stop," she told me and laughed and put her hand upon my arm, "is this true?"

I could only smile, of course, it wasn't a real question, because she knew it could not be answered, "How do I know if it's true?" We both found everything so funny by now. Whatever fell from the split in the ceiling to which her head was always turned, fell fast. "It's not the kind of thing that gets to be true or untrue. It's made to be true by the structure of the thing itself. We have built truth into it." This was funny at the time, I swear.

"Into what? The story?"

"More or less."

"You know," she told me after a pause, "I'm not sure it will ever be true again."

"Maybe not this, but something else will be," I laughed and she laughed and we drank wine and ate cheese. We had no idea what we were talking about.

for how long did the subject watch the bloody finger

When Eve was doing science studies for money—having sensors stuck to her head and getting her hair washed by research students, counting x's and o's, pressing buzzers, and recording words over and over and over and over for $5 to $3000 depending on her blood pressure and how much time she could put in and whether or not she smoked—she met a Taiwanese girl. The girl hosted a $10 study which was just a survey on products: coffee and wine, chocolate and books. Or maybe, it occurred to Eve years later, the study wasn't about what it purported to be about. In a series of small rooms, the girl asked Eve questions about products and consumption and then left her with a survey about the same things she had just asked; afterwards, the girl would return and they would talk about products again. In the third room while they talked and the girl held a pen near her face as her elbow rested on the table, Eve noticed that the index finger on the girl's right hand was coated in dried blood. The small feathery wrinkles on her finger were filled in deep red and speckled lighter along the surface. It made her skin look like scales and Eve saw and said nothing. She answered the questions and was paid $10 and left. Eve thought of the bloody finger. She thought the girl had stuck it up her cunt and forgotten to wash her hands.

ah shanda far di goyim

On a cool night, under an orange moon where friends and friends of friends spilled sangria, I met Miles, a middle-aged gay man accompanying his young boyfriend to a Sainte-Jean party. He nearly fell into the fire and hollered "Oy gevalt!" and caught himself and bowed extravagantly to hoots and applause. Surprised by the saying amongst mainly secular Catholics, I asked after his Yiddish and learned of his life with a Jewish wife and two Jewish children. Though he had never converted nor learned much of the ritual, he did live in proximity for 20 years or so and used the idioms freely and spoke with his hands and overanalyzed himself and had a large descending nose and veiled lids. When I looked at him to try to find the Roman Catholic roots he named, as if I could see them in his hair under the bad black dye, I noticed the way he looked away quickly between his phrases and mine; how he ended sentences and feigned distraction as though he was done and needed nothing else from me or from any interaction, and I asked myself if it was Jewish to search someone's eyes for approval as I do—and of course it isn't Jewish just because I do it, but if it were, I would have found his chink. "My wife, *meshuGOO*—let me tell you! She gets this little half-breed poodle, doesn't bother to train him, never even attempts it, and of course, he pisses all over the floor. For 11 years! 11 years that little *noodge Kahlua* pissing and shitting. She never trained him! And why didn't I? Well it was her dog!

He didn't listen to me for shit, even though I was the one scrubbing the floor, always, I was scrubbing the floor, what did Kahlua care? The little *pisher*. And you know, maybe if not for a speeding car and...well, poor Kahlua!—I'd still be in the closet in the suburbs. But I just *couldn't* after the accident—you know, it was the shock of it, the sudden change, and my wife, my *meshu*GOO wife, talking *right away* about getting another goddamn dog! I couldn't, I just couldn't imagine myself living this life, this *lie!* through another fucking poodle." Everyone was laughing now, his story was rambling and his hands were flying, his nasally voice floated above the fire and his garish clothing in blue and silver reflected the moonlight like a JAP under a disco ball, so when I said, "*Meshuge?*" with a correction to his Yiddish I was hardly qualified to make and wholly unsure about making, the small crowd shifted uneasily. I stood smug in the assertion, though he only shrugged, "Yeah, of course," and continued with his tale of Kahlua the mutt that broke the beard—soon to be a crowd favorite—while I studied his mug and wondered where I could find the French Canadian he said his father was. When he threw another log on the fire I searched his body for competence and used my antisemitic proofs derived from his clumsy hurl to flog my shrinking self. And when he whined about aching feet and knees and moaned over a back cracked from bending too swiftly while dropping the cut log into the fire and damping the flame to boos from the boys standing around, I shrunk further and wondered truly, which kind of fool was I.

Maury the Mensch

I remember the way my grandfather walked, how he hobbled on his bow-legs. Brown, bald, big lower-lip. Messed up teeth. Incisors at angles, jagged and sharp. Like my mother's teeth. I had one pulled so the teeth would sit straight, but they're still trying to poke out. He wore nearly transparent polo shirts, so thin, the material, trying hard to cover his hard round belly, like dressing a tire in toilet paper. Thick, square, tinted glasses obscured his bull frog eyes, my eyes, my mother's eyes.

I saw him for Greek food after being told he had brain cancer. He had scabs all over his bald head and I wondered if the scabs were related to the cancer. Like it was pushing out of him. He talked about baseball with my mother's brother, Marc, and asked me questions about art school, always followed up with, "Good, that's good."

We saw him in the palliative care home the week he died. We walked in the garden and my mother told him she had taken a tour of Israel. He said, "I didn't know you spoke Hebrew."

She said, "I don't."

It was a closed casket. The rabbi called him a *mensch* and my mother laughed. My father looked sharply to quiet her, and she lowered an eyebrow.

At the reception, my grandfather's brother Larry wept grotesquely and dragged around a beach towel to wipe his face. Larry asked me if I was writing a story about my grandfather while I sat in a cushy chair in the middle of the room drawing unskilled pictures of galloping horses, I snickered reflexively, "No."

"I can't believe they called him a *mensch*," my mother could be heard saying to everybody that asked how she was doing. My father ate tiny tuna sandwiches and talked to my mother's brother Marc about the Olympics and the economy. I followed my mother around the room with my eyes. She was eager, like a kid at a school dance who just got asked to go steady with some loser and she had to tell her best friend about it. I looked down, watching my ponies glide through loose ink wheat and snake filled grass scrawls that made a sound like the wind, like the ocean, like a hush. When I looked up my mother had marched off, my father had moved on to salmon and egg and international peacekeeping, and my Great Uncle Larry was asking everyone if they had seen the titanium watch he must have left in the bathroom, and "what kind of a place is this?"

I found my mother smoking outside with her estranged step-brother also named Marc, "Maury was a great man," he was saying, "I'm so sorry for your loss. For our loss."

My mother watched him for a dramatic second in this arrogant, dubious way she rarely but effectively staged. "Marc," she spoke to him like a teenager to a child, inhaled, squinted her eyes and blew smoke out of the corner of her mouth, "d'you remember that time you were supposed to meet your father at the lake? And you and your mother and brother drove four hours to upstate New York and when you got to the campsite there was a message at the front desk and your mother read it, and you all piled back into the car and drove four hours home? And she didn't say anything. It was dark when you got home and the house looked the same. But then you noticed that the piano was gone, and your father's rain boots were gone. You remember the brown and black rain boots.

And your Mother started crying. She cried when you moved into your grandparents' house, and she cried when she brought you to your new school. Do you remember, at all, not knowing where your father was, and all anyone would tell you was not to think about it and you couldn't figure out if you should be sad or mad or *what*—oh wait, wait, that was *me*. That was *my* father. That was Maury. Yeah. He was a real *mensch*."

Eulogy for the Man with the Trumpet

I didn't know my father. I'm not standing up here in front of you to complain about him. I just want to tell you what he means to me. I only have two stories, short—then we'll get the rabbi back up here. The first one, I was too young to remember but it was told to me by my late mother, who hated him. She rarely spoke of him but when she did it was bitterly—lost money, lost opportunities. She blamed him for things I won't go into, but you can imagine. Except—except when she told me the story about how he left. This she told with something like tenderness or sadness or wistfulness in her eye. She wasn't mad, so I thought I saw, she understood him through his tricks. Maybe that's what she hated about him—that she understood why he left, that everyone understood, that it was understandable, and that he did it anyway. It was different for me though. When I first heard the story, and I heard it many times after, I didn't understand it. I didn't have the life to understand it. It was a myth for me. And it helped me to make up who I thought the great man was. I came to think he was great, of course, because of the reasons everyone here thinks highly of him. Because of his work, his writing, his public life; the insight they say he had, the ability, the charm. But imagine *this* as your introduction. Imagine, or maybe you already know to see him this way—imagine his success as tragic and the man as a story. The first time I heard my mother's version of him, I half knew it, so I must have heard it before, but this was the first time I remember so the knowing was more like a fundamental knowing, not a conscious knowing—I hadn't been surprised by what she told me. We were driving back from the grocery store—I remember it was snowing heavily and we were moving slow in the old blue station wagon. And I must have brought it up—said something any kid would say, would hope for, perhaps, seeing their mother scared, pulling a brave face, trying to get home without crashing the car and what might happen if it did crash; how there was nothing beyond and she was always on the edge, not knowing how we might come down—I said something like, When is Daddy coming home? She looked at me and she smiled and called me Love. She said, Daddy isn't coming home. She told me, Your father—your father is not a fool, but he's fool enough to think he could get away with being crazy. He was selling insurance at the time, running a team and really working. He hadn't graduated high school, he didn't have experience; he'd worked his way up through hard sales and long hours—and she thought he did it for us. Other times she thought maybe he just needed to work, needed to move, needed to be absorbed by something so he didn't have to stop to look at his life and see the shape of it. He worked himself dumb and maybe when he looked at what he'd made it wasn't big enough to justify the effort. His whole life was insurance by the time I was born. He ran the place and he came home to us every night. He set up the routes for the salesmen, he sent them around to the counties, he led the team, I guess, that's what she told me. He'd come home each night looking tired and he never wanted to talk to about it. Sometimes she'd go find him at the office and try to take him out, to cheer him, but he was tired then too. And then one day he went to work early, without breakfast. He looked at his secretary Darlene and he told her, My feet are wet and they keep getting wetter. Then he ran out into the street, stopped a car with his hand held out flat like STOP, and tried to get into the driver's seat. The driver was still sitting there and he was just clambering all over her, trying to get in like she wasn't there. I can't remember the woman's name, my mother told me she spoke to her and neither understood what he was trying to do. It wasn't clear. He had no leverage. He was a desperate man, but what was he desperate about? She couldn't say what *he* thought he was doing either because when she went to see him in the hospital he said he didn't remember. He couldn't squeeze himself into the car I guess and he just sort of fell down on the street and had like, a seizure—though the doctor told my mother at the hospital—with my father resting in the other room—that the seizure had been *forced*. Forced? She asked the doctor, what does that mean? And the doctor told her that he'd *faked* it. She went in to see Wendell and he looked happy to see her—all woozy like he'd been on drugs, but they hadn't given him anything; he grabbed my mother's hand and told her that she was a really special person and then he threw his head backwards as though something had taken hold of him, as though he thought she'd think he'd just up and died. And my mother shouted, Wendell! What the hell! Wendell! And she shook him and could see his eyes struggling to stay shut and feel his body resisting and she said, You're faking it! The doctor said you faked that seizure and now you're faking this death, you're being crazy Wendell! And Wendell opened his eyes and looked up at her like he was playing at waking up to his own stupor and asked in a small voice why she was shaking him. She didn't believe him. She asked if he thought it was easy to fake insanity, epilepsy, and death. She knew he was still in there, she wouldn't believe that he wasn't in there. She told him, Wendell, I don't know what this is but I want you to snap out of it and I want you to come home. And she left him there in the hospital. She regretted that. She said she shouldn't have left. She said she should have stayed, should have worried, should have played his game. But she hated his game. So she came home; my father, he never came home. My mother went to see him the next morning and he was gone. The next time she heard about him was in the newspaper, something about the success of his most recent book, though she would never read it. She would tell me the story of his disappearance and we would laugh. We laughed at my father the farce, the farce who had left the family. There was something else to it. He hadn't hurt us, he'd left us the story. And while my mother could only occasionally see through the hassle of the life we were living without him, I thought he was a great comedian. I read his books; I've read everything he's ever written. I knew I could see the failed illusion in his words like crimes against himself. I could see through him and I loved that he persisted. He never dropped the act. And I never discussed it with him. By the time I'd tracked him down, I was free, I thought, of any fantasy of him. I had no illusions, but by my love of disillusion I'd made a new myth. I thought I needed to know him, I thought maybe he had something for me. But he didn't. He really didn't. He hardly knew me, though we had the same receding chin and the same small ears. He looked at me and needled in his seat. There was no great act. And I hated to see him squirm, to see him lowered. I begged for the sham, the charade, the dressed up nut who could *schnor* his way out of anywhere, but he wouldn't give it to me. And so I had to love him from afar, his work, his vision, his voice, the knowing, pushing, self-asserting fraud. So this, the final story, was really a gift for me. I know it was. His gift to me. I want to ask you all, everyone, do you know how my father died? Well of course you don't want to shout it out, but I know what you think, you think he died of stomach cancer in seclusion in the Northwest Territories, holed up in a shack, writing furiously through the pain, thinking of the frozen land and the whistle on the snow plains—and let me tell you—the truth is much better. I've got it now, I know what his press agent thought was beneath a great legacy and I'll share it with you today.

My father had been on a cruise ship in the Hawaiian islands with his new wife, Amber—she couldn't make it here today. I was told that they often danced around by the pool after lunch—lunch, a daily feast of wine and dishes like the Landlubbing London Broil, Prawns in Paradise, and what the staff said was my father's favorite, the Fantasy Al Forno. I spoke to a steward who said he'd once dropped a tray of the stuff and Wendell threw himself on the floor and shovelled it into his face to what maybe he assumed would be applause or squalid orgy but was instead just an awful embarrassment. The steward shrugged and told me, There was plenty more in the back. Amber, though, laughed shrilly at his open-mouthed antics and they roamed the vessel together. After lunch there would be a party on the deck and a DJ would blast top 40 jams and oldie hits over the Pacific; my father would shimmy shirtless in a pair of swim trunks and plastic flip flops amongst the tanned, oiled, age-hardened bodies. Often, over the course of the trip, he was seen wandering the deck, his face smeared with pasta sauce, trunks hanging low under his belly, a toothpick on the edge of his lips, or... you know, no toothpick. He died of peritonitis four days after the ship docked in Oahu. When I met him in the morgue, inexplicably, they still had him wearing a gold chain with the words *Amber Baby* nestled in the sun-bleached hair of his tanned chest. Afterwards, the autopsy revealed a small sharp piece of wood lodged in his abdomen. He'd swallowed a toothpick and died. And it's my favorite thing about him.

a timeless shrug

The short & swarthy man ambling awkwardly down the street, hunched from the cold, nose gifted from the Greeks persists because—what else do you do when it's cold but try to get home? —maybe he's a Jew.

Eli from that dating app who spent ten years in a mental hospital and wonders out loud why we're all so nervous,

"I don't think you can say that."

"But it seems true."

He's not neurotic, he likes, "TO THINK OF MYSELF AS ONE OF THOSE SEXPOET JEWS. LIKE LEONARD COHEN."

Cousin Al, bad skin, contrary tone, sitting on a dirty beige couch blaming his mother for giving him everything including the miniature mezuzah around his neck,

"Is there blood in it?"

"My history teacher told me 'of course not'."

—maybe he's a Jew, but has he had his DNA tested?

And Al's girlfriend, so pert and tidy, leaves the house like she's gathering kids from kindergarten for a hand-in-hand walk from the playground to the classroom, "Is everyone ready to go?"

—*shiksa*, I'm telling you.

Krumholtz & Me (a jellyfish)

The Science of Love on TLC made me think that I loved me. Take this female face and make it male—ideal. You love you, once removed, twice removed, at slight remove. Breed you to you—TV knows, TV knows what you do. Different enough to beat disease, but enough me that I get to see the polyps grow and make their own solipsoul. In each piece of DNA a ghostly outline, and each outline lives then dies then floats thereafter amongst its other—more tangible then he (though they thank him, immortal jellyfish of their blood), every other he that he met to make ye, young growth.

The *Addams Family Values* on TBS made me think that sickly asthmatic depressives were my heart's desire. Was I like the female face of little David Krumholtz, the child nebbish, effectual enough to play ineffectual in the movies, on TV; matching little you's to little me's through qualities serialized and love pangs of good timing? But he never found me and my polyps are me finding me and breeding the rhythms that were the love that made me think it was me as a male celebrity. And whoever finds whatever words generated by transdifferentiated me, picks up the outgrowth soul and reads.

L'Shana Tova, I Guess

It's Rosh Hashanah and my keyboard is sticky with honey.
Pomegranate juice has splattered the counter top.
Someone has to take out the fish bones.

It's been 5780 years since what.
The convert at the temple said we'd been going for so long.
The candle is not kosher, but it will burn.

"If there's a G-d," my mother would say, "HE would know."
HE would know
the heavy texts are not my heart

Thou Shall Feel Good
And Don't Worry About It

Who do I worry for
If HE knows my heart

For kind of a nice building
And ten smart men.

TV ח׳

Snorting unprincipled laughter watching children's movies made
for adults
in front of the TV in sweatpants, licking gravy from the plate,
eyes fixated on the opaque, crowded window
into places she is invited to observe only. but observe is all she wants.

For a Song

The old man sat there under the tall shelves looking like a sandbag slumped against a heavy door, holding it open, sliding incrementally forward until eventually pushed past the point at which it could maintain hold against the door—which closed, leaving the sandbag stuck between the door and the frame. When I walked in he looked up at me. I told him how interesting his store was. We looked around together, eyes travelling up and down the high shelves along the spines of the long forgotten, badly marketed board games. Thousands of deadstock board games in vacuumed plastic, growing older. The popular games had sold, and what remained were clunky safety games, *Don't Stop There!* public health games, *Smokers Wild*, and single note dice games like *Drive!*, *Can't!*, and *Ambulation!*, which took a player around a board towards an inevitable but uneventful win. The old man sat at a counter half the length of the warehouse on a swivel stool with his pudgy hands folded in his lap. I told him how I loved his store and my eyes spun around the room, along the shelves, and down the counter. He sighed. I walked through the shelves picking up strange new games featuring awkward would-be celebrities in hammy positions, in cheap costumes, hocking concepts. I laughed and gathered what I considered an amusing assortment: a game about drugs, *Don't You Dare*; a deck of cards for magicians or cheaters with an instructional video tape by Mordorlon, a moustache twizzler; and a calendar of stock photos of cats in seasonal gear. I asked the old man if he had an online shop, feeling awkward and sorry that I was the only person in the echoing game warehouse. He didn't, he told me. He wouldn't know where to begin, he told me. His son Gregory was supposed to help him get the shop online, they had discussed it, but Gregory was a very busy boy. I'm not sure if I was moved by Gregory's absence or I saw some kitsch value in this old man and his warehouse of unpopular past-times, but I was intrigued, I was sort of giddy, riding high on some impression I felt I was making with my wistful hopeful walk around the store. I was inspired, I asked him a thousand questions. Why did he have the games? Why wouldn't Gregory help? What about Gregory's mother? What about Gregory's sister? Did he know what a goldmine this old junk was? Did he need a sassy young upstart to pull this thing together? And on and on; I'd volunteered myself. A wife who'd "fallen off the face of the earth" and taken an old man's "hopes and dreams" wasn't even the "clincher." That's not what did the business in; what really did it wasn't any one thing. It wasn't the fact that his kids wanted to go to university, wanted bigger or better lives for themselves (what could be bigger or better than a warehouse chock full of other people's ideas?)—this business was for them! It was for them and their children and this was the legacy. There was no other legacy. Did Gregory and Wanda think there was an inheritance beyond this? This was it! And what could a person do with that? With an ill-conceived hope that persisted because nothing replaced it and it didn't know where to go. Well well well Gregory, well well well Wanda, it's nice that you've come back now that this aimless bitch has marketed the family game store, has made the family game store a hot new attraction in the world of not only game stores and toy stores but online stores and online worlds and as far as the internet goes, we made it, we had it all. Have you seen those old ladies dressed like club kids dancing and soothing their flaking skin with tween love and endorsements by fashion houses? Of course that is it, that is it. You should see how this junk looks to the young, to the new, the fresh thing we do, this is what needs to be done, take it to the next stage, the next level, bring this shit into it, if you know what I mean. I told the old man the plans for his store, I told him he didn't need a store, the store could fade beneath the WiFi waves washing up with the tides of a trillion young eyes, this was it, this was what I was going to do for him. And he might've let his family off the hook, he might've stopped for a second slouching and stood up and looked at me renewed. His eyes might've grown wide when I spoke of the megatons of public adoration and cash piles upon which he sat. We might've looked into each other's eyes and seen two separate things. I might've seen possibility become an old man behind a long counter, and good intention and a sound idea run fast and take shape as work and risk and wrenching failure and ignored success. Was this it? I thought to myself looking into the flies of hope circling the open can of a withered eyelid. He might've seen youth and possibility and his own dry plan soaked by what? Weeks of nourishing wet, he might've thought or seen—or not, hail, bouncing off, leaving dents. It was false. I knew myself to be untrue as I generated from my wriggling core, pulling whatever I found, every effort to be myself, every effort to make myself a person: snake oil in the blood, on the brain, through the nose from the air. I and we and the shape of the store and the space of the store made it seem like it couldn't be slick for how many shelves it had. We, the store and I, the old man and I, the I and I, utterly believed in me until I could see what I had done, what I had spun, and how much work for what possibility of success could be wrangled? I was a musical montage and when the song ends and the scene doesn't cut we find ourselves once again a silly girl and a sad man at a long counter, but which is which? Which is fucking which! Oy Gregory, isn't this your job? The toil not the song. Wanda, she never had any intention of helping. She so much knew that she hated the idea of the family business that she decided at an early age that she wouldn't play a fucking board game. She wouldn't play. He brought a new game home and Wanda would lock herself in the bathroom, turn on the hairdryer, and sit on the toilet. "I'm busy!" She's fucking busy Dad. So we were faced with it, the intractable part of the hope, remnants, swayed by a song, skewered daily. And so I did what any kid born under the bleachers at the Ice Capades would do, I paid for my games and held that fucking final note until the door closed behind me.

"Give it to me. I'll do it."

Sandy Shelley was really good at buttering matzo. She kept the butter in the fridge because she was afraid it would spoil so it was always too hard to use. Her daughter Gina would break the frail cracker into bits trying to butter it or just glob on lumps of butter and mash them around with her finger or eat mostly plain matzo with bursts of butter. Sandy would use the same cold butter as her daughter and spread it around carefully, never breaking the unleavened bread, making sure every inch was covered in a thin layer. Maybe owing to Gina's bad buttering or some innate quality, she liked the butter thicker. Sandy did it perfectly, but, Gina thought, a little thin. It didn't seem like it took her too long, like any longer than it took Gina, but she had more practice maybe, or like, adult hands. I don't know if Gina still can't cold butter matzo, 'cause she leaves her butter on the counter now and Sandy died suddenly, years ago.

Luftmentschen Living in Cloudy Places, Undoing Things

My brother-in-law Danny is an angry little man with a fat nose, rubbery pink skin, and blond hair. His teeth are piled up in his mouth and he has like a miniature pig presence. In a greedy small-minded way. He's always angry, he's always suffering some injustice. He's one of the most tedious people to endure. The family is together for the holidays and he counts time like he's being tortured. "At least today is half over," he says.

"I like holidays," I tell him, "I like reading and sleeping late and wearing sweatpants. I like watching movies with the cousins and drinking coffee all day." And it always surprises me that he's nice to me. If I was any other man who had said the very same thing, he'd have snapped in an irritable way that's designed to amuse the other men around him, and maybe assert his superior way of thinking, and/or even relieve some insecurity he holds about his whiny way of passing time—but when I say it, he laughs good-naturedly (almost) and 'lets me' have my opinion. I don't think he contributes much to the world, but I'm narrow in the things that I think are good. I like thoughts and ideas and words. And as far as practicality and functioning and efficiency, I'd like to leave that to experts. But he isn't one. An expert. He isn't an expert of anything. He's wrong about more things than any one person has a right to be wrong about. He is incessantly wrong. He's so wrong his words are floating garbage. He's pollution. But maybe I don't mind. He makes up the variety. Things explode for him. Sunglasses wrap-around faces and plastic bits float through river streams for him. He's okay with a life that isn't much and without people like that you'd just have a world of raving neurotics slyly biting each other on the shins to get ahead. People like forests where parasites kill trees and trees feed the floor and the dirt gets rich and dirt's as good as trees in the scheme of things.

Joke's on You

In the synagogue there was Stan, a filmmaker with a ponytail. A lovely serene man who wore, like a uniform, khaki cargo pants and a fleece vest. When the ceiling came down all he said was, "Ohhh Oh," and held his friend back, the very old one. So old he was gauzy. He was hunched in two over a walker. He must have been quite tall in his youth because bent over he was still as tall as most, and much more imposing. He took up double space this way. Height and width. A skeletal man with massive width and a squeaky walker. Sparse white wires jutted from his head indiscriminately—as much from his ears and nose and eyebrows as his scalp. Discus nostrils and a thin tip peaking between; thin and pointed as though everything around him was drawn towards that point—everything hung on the end of his nose and his nose wasn't big enough to hold it all. His voice when he wheeled up to read with the minyan was booming and nasal—like a projection with the settings askew. He sang out of turn also. The rabbi would call and wait for a response and the hunched man would always call. He was old though, over 90 and there was no need to stop him. No need until the ceiling fell and Stan held him back like a child in the front seat at a quick stop. Neither were hit, though the dust afterwards made the old man cough and Stan could be seen with his arm over the man's shoulders escorting him to the small equipment-laden bus that waited in the parking lot every Saturday.

There were three other walkers at the ends of the pews. None of them squeaked like that of the hunched and pinched man. But the three other walkers didn't look as old as his. One belonged to Lilian whose face was grey and who wore a floral dress with a crocheted kippah and tallit— all the women, even the very old women wore both kippahs and tallits at the synagogue. And Lilian made her own and those that her daughter Jill wore. Lilian and Jill looked identical. They sat next to each other like time was jumping. The other two walkers blocked the aisle which no one usually bothered about and only became a problem when the rabbi read from Ezekiel and the wheels started rolling—at least that's how the story would go after. There were only 12 or so people there for the service but more than half of them couldn't be counted upon to jump over the walkers in the aisle, though it didn't stop them from trying. Scattered limbs and fearful faces from every direction shouting, "Oh my god!" after they heard the ceiling rumble and wondered if they would survive. Then they wondered about punishment. Can you see a tangle of fragile bones and hollow aluminum stretched out before you under an amber glass Star of David and not wonder how your life has come to this? It was telling—though of what, no one could be sure—which is why when the wisecracking Cincinnati doctor shouted "God has spoken!" like he was getting the last laugh, and the South Asian convert cracked back, "But what did he say?" No one answered though there might have been a few chuckles if that hadn't been the same moment everyone saw that the lonely looking girl in the blue dress who'd shown up only that day, could not be seen. "She couldn't be under all that." "We'd see her. A foot or something." "I think she left." Well they had to dig, and dig quickly, because if she was under there, she might be suffocating and they'd have to save her. How come they didn't know? It made them wonder. The rabbi dug and the gabbai helped the two old women detangle their walkers from the one woman who was trying to get free and Jill dug, and Stan dug, though the old man couldn't be asked to help as bending over would have cracked his back, crack! That was the sound they heard and the rabbi had blamed the weather—though had they thought about it they would have wondered, as it hadn't been cloudy—though weather changes, weather is changeable, and the crack sounded if not like the weather then the crack of a whip or the crack of a back from inside your own body. So no one expected the hunched old man to help dig out the new girl if she was even under there, though the Cincinnati doctor assured everyone that she wasn't, "She left! I'm sure!" While his wife stood by his side looking like it wasn't worth the headache later bringing up the doubt she felt in him right then. And they dug and the words replayed in their minds, taking on more gravity than the irreverent levity with which they'd been uttered, "God has spoken!" "But what did he say?" The rabbi didn't let on through his digging, pushing aside drywall pebbles and twisted scraps of painted metal, that he was trying to frame this, trying to parse this, trying to get a sense of how he could spin the tragedy if it was a tragedy or uplift the congregants if they'd all been spared, though he chastised himself for thinking of anything other than the girl while he dug and Stan dug and Jill and the gabbai now all dug. And only the very elderly or very certain stood by, unsure. And it was odd that no one thought to call emergency services until eventually, they did. There was something isolating about the cave-in. The congregants all felt in that moment as though they were the only people in the world. To call the ambulance, had it occurred to them, which it didn't until they found the shoes, would have made them unclean, impure, and unable to remain standing before each other in the synagogue amongst the debris of a partially caved-in ceiling. They felt spared, though it isn't something you can say—besides, it all happened so quickly. And the shoes! The shoes convinced them something worse was happening. The Cincinnati doctor said, "It's a trick!" And the gabbai ran to call for help and the elderly started to filter out of the synagogue, it was too much, they could be heard to say, it was all too much.

And of course, they weren't her shoes at all, but just some shoes that had been left under the pew. You know, maybe they were her shoes, but there was no body, the fire department concluded, and so nothing was so tragic. "Who would leave their shoes behind?" said the South Asian convert named Isaiah, who mentioned when he told you his name was Isaiah that it was an assumed name, one he'd taken when he converted, and curious, one thought when hearing the admission, that he would have mentioned the change at all, which otherwise wouldn't have been wondered about, but when Isaiah said, "Who would leave their shoes behind!" and embodied the relief and the head shaking disbelief of the fact of it and fed a hastening of their escape, as it had been occurring in the panic of the search that the rest of the roof could fall at any time, when he said, "Who would leave their shoes behind!" the Cincinnati doctor could be heard to shout to the few folks who were left and the firemen who were pushing them out, "At least the shoes didn't leave her behind!" Though no one was heard to laugh.

eyelids askance; knows best

"Oh. Well, you never know what will happen," my grandmother said when I told her I planned to open a bagel business in Northern BC. And whether the business flies or fails she will not need to tell me that she told me so.

Please Don't Eat That

I can't stomach a food court sticky and thick with smells of fries and spring rolls and muddy feet and sweaty faces. It's a terrible place to take a date—worse, if you plan to scour the tables for half-empty soup bowls and hard buns, though I can't imagine why anyone would. I can't imagine. It shouldn't be hard to imagine the person I was only ten years ago but maybe—no—I was going to say, maybe I'm too far from that person now—or maybe I've detached myself—but that gives me too much credit for growth or progress. Like I'm so far removed. Like I can't be held responsible. The truth, what's the truth? It didn't gross me out—and it only disgusts me now through creeping shame, through failure forcing me to see that maybe when he stood stiffly by and watched me slurp something wet from a brown plastic tray, maybe that face he made was disapproval. But then I could only see free burritos and discarded sandwiches. And free made me feel like I was doing alright. The old crusted moustache sipping soup till he got sick of it and ambling out of the basement food court with another thing planned was as far from me as the beakless chicken bred extra fatty. It was food. Caleb, who's a chef now—maybe that's why he squished up his nose like he was on a date with a trash-eater while he was on a date with a trash-eater—Caleb didn't seem to see it that way. But I mean, all the punks in Montreal dumpster dived, so it wasn't the farthest thing from whatever kind of lives we were living. The Atwater dumpster felt cleaner than the average trash can and that was the hot spot, but I'm sure he spent time in the Aubut dumpster too fishing for freshly expired yogurt from under cardboard boxes soaked with sour orange juice. I'm sure.

There were other things though. Two main other things. Three main other things. There was the time I had a date at the free McGill movie night put on by the Neuroscience Department where they would link the movie to some kind of brain issue and get a doctor to speak on the things he knew about brains. I had a date but it was more of a friend-date and Michael was late, quite late, and I thought maybe he wasn't coming so I saw Caleb sitting in the front row and I went to sit with him. Hello I said. I was stood up I said. The movie had started and he didn't make much reply. Sort of a Oh I see Hm Hm. And we watched, maybe some normal things were said. Ha ha, look at him go about the movie, which might have been Young Frankenstein. And then Michael showed up and he was so late and he had snot dripping from his face from the cold as he had biked; he biked even in winter. And he, Michael, beneath the broken brain of Saint Delbruck, inexplicably sat on the other side of Caleb. So our date, not so much a date but Caleb didn't know to what extent it was a date—our date surrounded him. And Michael's comments to me were filtered through Caleb and my comments to Michael were filtered through Caleb. And Caleb sat stiffly and I considered that maybe it was odd so I tried to do what people sometimes do which is make it *light*, make it *normal*, with smiles and pats and loud laughs at old jokes. And I thought I did. And we all left together somehow. Michael remaining on the wrong side of Caleb and me trying to act upbeat as though we were having a great time and then on the walk through campus Caleb said, I have to go. I have something to do in my office which is nearby. Goodbye he said. And I thought little of it at the time, I didn't consider that it was late, maybe 11 and he most likely had no work, had no meeting in his office at that hour. Most likely.

So there's that, and then there's this: Caleb was once loved by a talented woman, a woman I knew who drew pen drawings of strangers and the drawings were not made to be real but she always captured something in their face that made it more than a cartoon. She loved him. And I could see when we all met that he didn't love her. I could see that he looked like my ex-boyfriend, that he looked like my future boyfriend. That he had a face that could have loved me. He was the type that always loved me. And he tried. He invited me places. Like once to a bar and I was an hour late and he was still there reading a book like Jean Rhys or Joan Didion or something and I had been crying hysterically over a man I loved who would never love me who didn't have a face I could recognize as someone who could ever love me, and me *my* face was red and puffed up but I thought I'd covered it with enough pale makeup to make myself presentable. I hadn't. His look of shock. Caleb's. I remember it now. I didn't know it would stick. And what was worse maybe than all of this, is that when I did try to know him, know Caleb, I couldn't really make him know me and so I never really knew what he could like about me, except that I had dated men like him. Men who I had been good around. Men who I could see what they liked in me because I was being a really good version of me. And maybe both Caleb and I expected that. But we couldn't connect. And I don't want to think it was because he was smarter than me, but maybe it was. Or maybe something about how we were emotionally—that's a nicer thought—out of sync. Like I can see the lower level food court in the underground mall—Caleb standing in the moat before the pool of laminate tables and chairs while I showed him what we could get for free—what kind of people we could be if it didn't matter what kind of people we were. And while I couldn't see them then, I could draw the lines around his nose now—animated in my memory: the small change in his face and the slight change in my ease that made me less funny, less intelligent, less in the pocket, on the ball, round the corner, up the street, fuel the car, fill the tank, round the bend, then I thought I could be. Like I wasn't the best me with him. And so I didn't love him. But think how different things might be if he just would have eaten the garbage.

PIG MEAT

Jane's attempt to seduce the rabbi failed when he found a pork bun in her purse. The Chinese bakery six blocks from the synagogue was open at 10:00 AM and Jane couldn't resist an open door filled with pastry and pork meat. She stepped in and swallowed a shrimp spring roll and bought a bun for her walk to the synagogue for a Hebrew lesson she'd arranged—late in life, she thought the congregants thought.

A sign on the door with golden letters prohibited outside food, so she stuck the remainder of the bun in her purse and snuck it through. And though she dressed modestly for her first private lesson, the bun in her bag said meat, and the sweet pig and full blown bottom-feeder on her breath made even her black dress look like sacrilege. So in the small yellow and white walled room, postered with pencil mascots and star-shaped cheers, young but not too young Jane pulled the silver-haired gapped-tooth rabbi—looking like an aging soap star, smelling of aftershave and his wife's potpourri—towards her unholy mouth before he sniffed and she asked, "Does my breath smell?"

He, with his right hand on the small of her back, dug his left hand into the gap in her sloppy purse and pulled out a crunched-up half-chewed shredded BBQ pork bun. He held it up and gave his head a small tsk-ing shake before coolly removing himself from her within her little arms which lifted as she shrugged and snatched back the bun. "I'm still learning," she snapped.

Lizard People

Last night I was telling Liz and Nick about this thing with Beth and Trevor. I didn't think it was such a great story and I kept qualifying it like, "I probably shouldn't be telling this story." Because just because it made me think of this time I betrayed a nice man in a bad suit. I was working at the Paramount under the name Lorelei Lee—after Marilyn Monroe in *Gentlemen Prefer Blondes* because I thought she had the best line, "Don't you know that a man being rich is like a girl being pretty?" And I always forgot the end of it, something like, "You wouldn't marry a girl just because she's pretty but it doesn't hurt." I would kind of make up my own second sentence like, "It isn't everything, but it doesn't hurt." I'd tell guys the story when they asked what my real name was and sort of distract them or tell it in a way that would make them laugh. And one night I met this blond man with cherubic cheeks and wet worried eyes. His suit looked too big and he seemed so small. He told me he never normally comes to places like this, and he doesn't know if it's the right place for him, then he told me he had a secret and he made me swear to never tell anyone. And he was like any other guy in the place, I mean you can like them or notice that they have funny qualities like a big suit and the morality of a 12-year-old boy in a movie about the 1950s where he finds like a porno collection and looks at it tenderly, appreciatively, fearfully, but you'll also tell them whatever they want to hear, that's the hustle, everyone knows the hustle, or at least you think they sort of do. Anyway it doesn't excuse my behavior, though it feels like I'm trying to, I suppose I'm really just trying to think of reasons I did it. But he tells me in a whisper with his eyes pointed down and his face turning red that he would like to see my feet. And I laughed and I was like, "Sure!" Feet guys were O.K. with me, I found them gentle for the most part, respectful, with a real love of worship. Anyway he begged me again not to tell when I told him I had to go do my stage routine and I said, "Yeah of course, sure." And he asked me to meet him at the bar afterwards and I was like, "Sure, sounds good." And I went to the back where all the girls sat in front of the big mirror behind the stage—the Paramount was cool, it was an old theatre, so the stage smelled like a stage and had curtains like a stage and tall ceilings and dark corners and a basement full of marquee letters. And all the girls sat at the long mirror, a mirror the width of the building, putting on beautiful makeup like sparkly makeup and giant eyelashes and they sat there smoking too. I picked a paisley kind of loose synthetic silk dress out of my locker, one with a high neck and no sleeves, I was thinking of the foot fetish guy too, I don't know why, it just felt like an outfit that he would like. And I danced to a Fleetwood Mac song, or maybe it was Stevie Nicks, anyway it had her voice, and I always danced to that voice when I wore that dress and I'd just learned a new foot move that two of the girls said was much better than anything I'd ever done before, which made me think it was kind of backhanded compliment, but not untrue as I was generally really uncoordinated in life and dancing around on six inch patent plastic platform heels was a feat for me. So I was happy dancing, liking the song and the dress and the lacy black underwear that snapped off—the stage routine was everybody's favorite part; you got to be on stage in pretty things dancing and singing along (they told me to stop singing along but why would I?) and feeling like people wanted to look at you, at all of you, they didn't even just want to look at you, they wanted to possess you, to hold you, to spend money on you. Anything they could do to you, they wanted to do it, and I liked the feeling. Especially from the stage where no one ever got close enough to complicate the nice life with their hang ups. Afterwards in the dressing room fixing my makeup and picking a good floor outfit for the foot fetish guy, I told Skyler who was sitting next to me with her straight blond bob and aquiline nose, with her perfect fake tits and orange-brown skin, that I had a foot fetish guy waiting for me and he was so shy and cute. Skyler laughed and we talked about how sweet foot fetish guys were, not like we were experts, but it was backstage talk, we weren't best friends, so we said things that were basic and easy like about how sweet foot fetishists were. Then I came down the stairs on the right hand side of the stage and I saw the blond man in the suit sitting at the bar watching me and occasionally bringing his hand to his forehead like wiping the sweat or clearing his hair away or just for the feeling of a hard push against your forehead. Then I saw my friend Ivy and she was sitting with the long-haired Chinese guy who wore small round glasses, smoked, and didn't say much. She flagged me down and asked what I was doing for food, and I told her I had to go I had a foot fetish guy waiting and he was right up at the bar looking so sweet and cute with his big suit and small shiny shoes and she laughed and looked back at him then we said maybe we'd get sushi later and the Chinese guy didn't mind what Ivy did or said or if she even paid attention to him, just as long as she was there with him he'd slip her quiet $20s every 10 minutes till he'd get up, shake her hand, and just leave without ever really saying anything. She liked him so much and everyone was always jealous of those kinds of set-ups but he wouldn't talk to anyone except Ivy. One night when she was home sick or something he took a different blond, Jasmin, to a backroom for a dance and as soon as she was done he left. With Ivy he'd stay for about an hour or two and this was only three and a half minutes and he never took another girl after that. But I left her sitting with the quiet guy and they both looked straight ahead at the stage. Then I started up to the bar but I stopped quick again when the waitress asked me if the last guy I was with bought me a drink 'cause she didn't write it down and I said he did and then we laughed like people do when they just say normal things so that it doesn't get tedious just walking around talking to people forever. And I walked towards the bar where the blond cherubic man with the big lazy suit and little teeny tiny shiny shoes was sitting with his head completely collapsed in his hands and I said, "Hey." And he looked up like he was startled and said that he *loved* my stage routine, he *loved* it, and he *loved* the dress I wore and the shoes and even the song, he gushed until I felt really good about myself then he said he had to go to the washroom. And he ran towards the door looking like he was pulling up his pants and brushing his hair at the same time, and he had a look on his face like he'd seen a ghost or a bunch of ghosts or he was used to seeing ghosts but he wasn't used to them talking, and then he ran right out and I never saw him again. And at first I was really confused, like I thought maybe he was just a weird liar, or messed up in the head or something. And then it sort of creeped over me, this feeling like I was an evil sinner, like I was a Godless, heartless temptress who couldn't be trusted and there was a hell and I was going or maybe I was in it and I was just reliving that moment of realization over and over forever and all the sick gross feelings that came with it.

When I told Liz and Nick about Beth and Trevor, I thought about the blond man in the big suit, but either I was desensitized, or Beth and Trevor aren't little angels of the strip club so I'm not the little devil that sits opposite, or Nick laughing and shouting, "Are you serious?" outweighed any feelings I'd had about Beth and Trevor. Because they were just two dumb kids, and they didn't beg me anything and they didn't trust me anything and they just apparently both had a crush on me and ditched me because I was coming between them. And when I read Beth's text out loud to Liz and Nick saying, "I probably shouldn't be telling this story," I kept *telling* the story, the story about how Beth and Trevor were entrapping me in this private little drama, but I didn't ask for it or know about it, or even invite myself over. I just played music with them sometimes and I could feel them both looking at me in that way and I knew they didn't get out much so I tried to remain in this plain space with like an air of professional friend, and when they both stopped talking to me altogether I half figured it was some twisted isolation that drove them to think weird thoughts about me. And then Beth confirmed it, telling me she owed me an explanation and when she wrote that I got like a tingling, like something sordid was being revealed and I was the king of all gossips, and she said they both felt something for me and how it came between them and I said no problemo and half forgot about it and wouldn't have even told the story if Beth hadn't sent me a panicked text later saying that she had told Trevor that she had told me and he wanted to see the conversation and she deleted the conversation and he was going to think that was suspicious so she wanted me to recreate the conversation with her and she was scared that he was cheating on her. And I just said that he probably wasn't cheating because he was sort of worthless and she was really much better than him and left it at that. And I told the last part in a frenzy, the part about Beth and the recreating the message and I threw in a bit about how Beth and Trevor killed a lizard because they were incompetent and his sad cage was too small and how the lizard deserved much more and Nick shouted, "That's insane!" and Liz looked at me like a little jealous she wasn't the one telling a good story about a dead lizard but still like she was happy to be hearing it, just with that okay this is funny face and I felt totally okay with telling Liz and Nick all about Beth and Trevor and their poor dead lizard, but I wouldn't have told them, any of them, about the man in the dishevelled suit that I betrayed in a strip club even though I was thinking it the whole time.

Crowded Rooms

Josephine holds the leash taut then yanks and kicks the dog—no, she would never. She walks past grass and figurines decorating happy grandparents' lawns and closes her eyes for one second under the sun and the dog pulls her into traffic and they die together in front of her own grandmother's house—her grandmother races outside after hearing a noise and trips on a horse like a kite planted in her yard and wails, "Oh my Josephine!" But of course Josephine isn't in the same city as her grandmother and so shakes her head quickly to retrain her thoughts and forgets for less than a second what city she's in. The dog tugs and pulls and Josephine screams "Aleister, Tara, Winston, Freddy—Freddy! Please!" Running through a short list of dead dogs and one cat (Winston) known from the time she was born (Aleister was ten at the time and she remembers him mainly from pictures and also, slightly, the gritty thickness of the fur near his skin) to her eleventh birthday (Tara from the SPCA who never broke the habit of peeing happily and showing off her belly whenever she met someone at the door) to her 26th year in an apartment with a chain-smoking webcam girl who takes in strays and forgets to bother over them after. Josephine shouts again "Freddy! Please!" As Freddy tugs and whines and screams and arrooo's like a husky because he wants to chase a jackrabbit who runs across the street and gets clipped by a motorcycle that spins out and flips over both her and Freddy—Freddy who's thinking, Josephine thought, *if he thought*, that it was a good thing he wasn't allowed to chase that jackrabbit. And they turn the corner, having almost made it home on the early morning walk, the one before breakfast, before coffee—saving those things like life's little treats, deferring, deferring eating until the need gives way to a gluttonous impulse so great Josephine overpays for Canadian-Chinese chicken balls and sweet red sauce and watery wonton soup while stuffing and bitching about herself doing both; she defers and defers until everything is life's little treat, the shower in the evening, the bed at 6AM, and depriving herself of sleep so that she may love to sleep later, after the dog gets walked—she begins to drift over the sinkholes she makes with each heavy step and the neighbours drown in pebbles with hands reaching out of tarred over roads along the suburban street fenced by the bones growing from the grassy patches of the route she takes only every other day because to take it too often would be saving nothing for later, when, it might have been nicer to take another route. *So you see*, she thinks to herself, lighting a cigarette and coughing, *life's lessons look like living much worse in order to take comfort in anything better*. "Is that true?" she asks herself out loud and Freddy looks at her quickly then darts his eyes away, without the ability to be interested.

Who's There

Jesus Christ. My roommate is downstairs chopping something and I can only assume from the sounds that her hair is flying and her arms are flailing. There's a bump and the house shivers. She's listening to alt-rock and preachy podcasts. Her boyfriend comes home and they squeal at each other. He slaps her ass and they scream and tear down the house. It's mayhem. He coughs, he hacks, he hoarks something. They cover the remnants of the living room, the kitchen, the unused dining room, in a layer of low-lying grey smoke. Shuffling closer and closer to my door I will it away and it works. Slams a door and marches again down the stairs and familiar sounds from familiar lives drift back upwards towards my own sealed off, shut in, creaky-hinged hollow. Scraping the dust with her slippers, she must have forgotten something else until she's calling from outside the door, "Gloria! Hey! Gloria!" My ears are ringing from the chaos of every other life I've watched lived and all the years I watched them live it, "What Ma?"

Strangers in the Vent

I understand why someone would murder the Russian girl in the adjacent apartment just for cutting her food rhythmically. She doesn't cut rhythmically at regular hours, she cuts rhythmically at irregular hours which is worse than if she cut rhythmically regularly obviously. 2AM, 8AM, 4PM, 732PM, she eats when she's hungry and she cuts her food into, presumably, small squares which she hardly has to chew because the squares are so small. She doesn't crunch, you would hear her crunch, she just cuts her food, saws at it, slices, and swallows. Metal to porcelain cleek, cleek, cleek. When you hear the plate scrape you know it's over but by then you hear every other small noise in the world like it were being played for you: the birds like a fraying cassette tape, the cat on the roof rolling, arching and cowling in heat, the incessant bandsaw of suburban Saskatchewan, and the Russian again, while she washes her dishes and the smell of a cheap orange scented dish soap flits through the vent and you are forced to recognize yet another aspect of her life. Lighting incense, sandalwood, and finding that it doesn't work to drown the stink of the life that moves methodically when it goes and erratically when it halts—what does she do in silence for 18 hours a day?—you open the window and risk the moths at the light until the moths fly at the light and you realize that your life is the real fucking mistake. Swatting at the dusty confused insects you knock your freaking glass lamp shade off the light on the ceiling and it crashes to the ground, missing your head—but you know what doesn't miss your head? The bodies of the dead brethren of the accursed moth you let in with your spite games—why play a game with a girl who isn't looking? Who can answer? Not her— those moth bodies are multitudinous, multitudinous! They're everywhere, all over your head and shoulders, they're in your hair and getting in your eyes! And the glass has shattered all over the floor. You, barefooted fool with eyes of bug dust step carefully and find your runners at the door and wipe your face on a jacket. GOOD FUCKING LORD you shout at no one, because there is no one, the sounds from next door having utterly ceased. Does she read quietly? Does she sleep when she isn't eating? Like a cat curled up against the window? Well, there's one way to find out, storm the damn vent that plays the sounds of her eating like a stereo speaker, then push your moth covered body through with a dustpan full of glass and dump that in her orange smelling sink or on her orange smelling head—why would she put dish soap in her hair? Who knows with these cutlery obsessed Russian day sleepers. You would know. You would know the life that sounds like scrapes by a vent and smells of cheap orange dish soap, and she would know—she would know exactly what kinds of things she makes you do.

plain as the nose

"I was standing at a bus stop on East Hastings at three in the morning and a Jewish looking girl— "

"You can't look Jewish," Georgia's gentile father interrupted, shaking his head and fanning emphatically the fingers on his left hand.

"Well she did. Anyway, this Jewish looking girl came up to me and asked me if I was Jewish. I said I was and she handed me this piece of paper and said I should look up this organization for a free trip to Israel."

Gary nodded, bent his neck, rolled his head to one side, and Fran said, "Oh, I've heard of these things. You work on a *kibbutz*. Will you go?"

Which Georgia dismissed as besides the point, "Yeah Ma, I mean, I'll look into it, I want a free trip—but don't you think that's *something*? That she just came up and asked me like that?"

Gary shrugged up to his head shaking, eyes closing, and Fran cooed, "Ohh yes, very funny!"

"Actually," Georgia pushed past her parents' unformed uneasiness, thinking she thought she heard in the distance maybe, some mass of wily wanderers, cats probably, hiss and scratch at the lamp post, "I thought I could tell a Jew, you know? I mean, *Uncle Ira—* "

"You can't look Jewish," Gary said.

She went on, angling towards her mother but keeping something, an eyeball, a backwards eye on Gary, "I thought maybe I could tell, like the girl at the bus stop could tell; like how some of our family—"

"*I* had it taken care of," Fran laughed and petted her nose.

Georgia snorted. "So then I ran into this *other* girl, very cute girl, in the bathroom of a bar. We were drunk, laughing and sort of bonding over costumes—she was the paper bag princess and I had blood smeared all over my face—and I looked at her frizzy hair, bulbous nose, and bullfrog eyes, and I asked, 'Are you Jewish?' And I expected she would say *yes*, of course, though I didn't think—I wouldn't have asked— but she just *looked* at me—"

Fran laughed through her ski-slope nose, pursed her lips, eyeballed Gary and shrugged a single shoulder while Gary glanced at Georgia's half empty glass then stared at the lake out of the restaurant window thinking of fishing, wondering if they stock this lake.

"And she was like, 'I'm Orthodox.' And I'm like, '...Orthodox...*Jew?*' and the girl in the paper bag dress tells me—says *stiffly*, 'NO. Eastern Orthodox.' And sort of quickly, but politely, I mean she was *polite*, leaves the bathroom."

Fran said, "Hm," and shifted in her seat. Gary raised his eyebrows and looked around the restaurant and bobbed his head rhythmically in a way where if he was an isolated figure you might think he was doing neck exercises for a sagging chin, like he had taken up face yoga because he was getting old and self-conscious but in this context, sitting with his family at a lakeside restaurant, he was just moving the conversation along, maybe not totally interested, maybe choosing disinterest, because—why Gary? Georgia went on, clearly sloshy, "So, I don't know, I mean, I know you can't *look* Jewish, but you can, right? And she did, but she wasn't, and I feel like I actually *upset* her—"

"Maybe she thought you were telling her she had a big nose," Fran said cutely. Gary cleared his throat.

"I guess. I mean, I didn't take it as an insult when the girl at the bus stop asked me. I thought she was, like, *magic*—I felt like I'd been asked to go to *wizarding* school!" Georgia and her mother cackled obscenely and threw their little fists down upon the glass table, shaking the silverware and quoting movie lines about wizardry under their breaths, under their breeths, settling suddenly when Gary BLEW, "That doesn't make any sense! How can you look Jewish? You can't *look* like a religion! And why would you want to? It's prejudice. You sound so... wrong. So wrong."

Georgia downed the last of her double and choked on some celery salt, "Yer just jealous," she drawled absurdly, "ya *goy*."

CLAY DATE

Alan took Serena to an old brick factory where they no longer made bricks. He stopped the long Cutlass with the cushy seats in a gravel parking lot and got out. His aged cowboy boots let pebbles in through the soles. It was hot and Serena wore a coral-coloured summer dress she'd considered in the mirror after trying on several others. She matched her shoes and left a pile of dresses and a scattering of sunglasses in her room on her bed and draped over the vanity. Alan rolled a joint on the back of the car and Serena pulled out oversized sunglasses and used her hand to block the sun that broke through the top and in at the edges. The day seemed sparse. The air was dry and the hills of clay that surrounded the brick factory were low and naked white. The small bushes that grew over the hills were covered in a clay silt; the glint of the buried green and the shock of the white clay was glitter under the sun that hissed like a steam kettle as water was sucked into the air. Alan didn't offer Serena anything to smoke. He wasn't used to offering. Serena wouldn't have taken any but not being offered had made her feel alone. They wandered the site, walking up the clay hills and shaking the black flies out of their hair. Serena wished she'd worn runners not sandals. Alan found some crystals in a rocky part of the hill and swore that the crystals used to be bigger when he was younger. Serena nodded and took a sip of luke-warm beer. He drank whisky from a flask and she asked for some and they passed the beer and the whiskey back and forth until they didn't feel the weight of the sun. They walked in the old factory and glanced at the signs. In the cafe afterwards Serena ordered a coffee and Alan ordered tomato soup all flat and red and it stuck in his moustache and he sucked it off noisily. Serena closed her eyes in the car and sighed. On the road Alan drove fast and took long, wide swerves as though he were falling asleep; she looked over at him and he looked back at her and smiled painfully. She looked away quickly thinking that she'd rather fly into a ditch than give this guy the wrong idea. Let him swerve.

"Did you have fun?" he asked in front of the long grass of her old house over the tape player loudly shouting out Kenny and Dolly. "Yeah, for sure. Thank you for taking me."

"Listen why don't we get a drink—"

" —Later this week?" she interrupted, "I'll give you a call."

He likes all the things I like. She wrote in a faux-leather bound notebook, *He took me to beautiful clay fields and picked crystals from the rocks. We listened to country music on cassette tapes on long, straight Saskatchewan roads and if I was writing the story of us I'd be in love.*

till the end

The sky was falling and her mind was racing. She could hear the debris hitting the roof and echoing through the house. She turned up the radio and picked out a pink thing to wear; when the radio became a blown out static trap of squandered voices she went to the bathroom to tease her hair and paint an outline of her face over her face. She might as well go out, her house wouldn't be there much longer.

INVITATIONS

Before a help wanted sign, like before death,
   my life flashes before my eyes.
   7AM on the bus.
   9AM on the phones.
   11:45 in the lunchroom.
   Sandra and I have an easy rapport but no friendship develops.
   At the Christmas party I fuck Jared from accounts receivable in the women's washroom on the fourth floor.
   On the first Monday of the New Year, he tells me he's leaving his wife.
   His daughter is old enough now; she won't care.
   She won't miss him.
   I arrive late. I work through lunches. I leave early.
   I stop answering my phone.

Before a help wanted sign, like before death,
   my life flashes before my eyes.

Heart to Heart

A 30-something woman sat on a train to Ottawa. She sat and thought of her mother's views on trains and planes. "It's like a mini vacation, like a vacation within a vacation," her mother would say. On the train, on the plane, you weren't expected to be anywhere but on the train, on the plane. This is where her mother could relax. This was guilt-free indulgence in TV, in movies, in scrolling the lists of content invented for distraction or clicks or for something else, no one is really sure. The woman on the train didn't find relief in trains, in planes, she found the trap of her mind and the places it would go and the inability to walk it out of her soul. She particularly hated planes. She thought terrible things. She scowled at the people around her, they moved too slow, they moved without regard for her or anyone else. They took up space without awareness of their jutting bodies. She hated them and thought the worst things she could think about them. She thought in slurs and reproached herself. Trains were stressful, planes were more. She had lines forming around her mouth and down the center of her forehead. But the lines hadn't displaced her features, not yet. She sat on the train travelling towards her childhood home and tried to silence her mind by thinking of the sound of the wheels on the rails and the smell of her parents' house and the babble of the televisions within, one from the kitchen, one from the living room, one, perhaps, in her mother's bathroom had been left on. The cold aerosol-spray smell of the train distracted her from distraction. She fidgeted. She turned towards the window and saw a hag in the trees. There was a moment when she couldn't place herself on the train and she couldn't understand the hag hovering in the green. She groped around her mind for order, for position. She tried to remember who she was but there was nothing to remember. She had gone, there was only the image of the hag, like a dream, accepted and real, but without context. It occurred to her in the heap of her mess-mind that she was seeing into the future. She could locate herself now but she could only barely locate the hag in the window. How many years in the future? How long until she met the hag whose heavy, wrinkled skin moped beneath its own gravity? What did the hag want, now, with this visit? She searched her mind again, a mind that was slowly reforming into known shapes and there she found a reference, under lore. There had been an old woman she'd heard of. An old woman who was very poor and who had a dream to one day see the inside of a hotel. It was a small dream. For a year this woman saved. And at the end of the year she was able to afford a single night in a hotel room. She walked into her temporary room and there she met a dirty little perturbed woman. She returned to the desk and told the concierge that if he insisted on her sharing the room, she would prefer a friendly woman. The concierge realized then that this poor woman had never seen her own reflection. And he told the woman, "A face answers to a face in water." The woman went away dwelling on the face in water, the face in water—when she again saw the old woman in her room, she smiled at her and received a smile in return. On the train then, with the wind whips of trees flying behind electric locomoted time, the woman who sat smiled to the hag in the window and saw the smile in return, a green grassy smile of the countryside beyond. Re-adjusting herself to her real future, and dismissing the magical years of manifested thought to come, she let the smile drip down her face and reminded herself while pulling open her purse and digging desperately for lipstick, that the middle man was glass and the image was not true.

PROVERBIAL

Many years ago, after having been thrown over by an ugly man of unparalleled integrity, I wandered the streets in a parody of my own misery, hair tangled, eyes swollen, shoulders rolled over. I gawked at passers-by with accusatory disgust. I snatched an apple from an outdoor vendor, took a bite, and let the fruit roll along the sidewalk. I shuffled along waiting for something. In front of an all-you-can-eat Chinese food buffet a Chinese man sat before a roughly written sign. The sign was red and the marker was black and dull and scribbled over and over to give weight to the letters. FORTUNE $10. It was cheap. The man before the sign was old and fitting. This was what I had wandered for; my aimless mooning about, weeping on street corners, making a montage of heartbreak, had led to this ancient wisdom about to be imparted. I sat in front of the old man and put down two blue fives. He creaked slowly and fluidly; his eyes washed over me as though bored by what we would discuss. He dropped the money in a jar and with the same languid movement took my hand. He looked at my palm and I looked at his eyes. They were jaundiced and crystallized. Whatever disease gave him golden eyes, it worked in his favor. I knew I would hear the truth. He said, "Your pinky finger, it grows to the side. You will be married after the age of 35." I replotted my life. He said, "Never cross a bridge. They're dangerous for you." I nodded but said nothing. He said, "Don't ever eat sushi. Not even Japanese people eat sushi." I nodded again, though I was having a hard time with the redesign: bridgeless, married, avoiding fish. He reached into the pocket of a pair of stained khaki pants and pulled out a neatly folded piece of red paper. He said, "Read it later." I thanked him excessively and walked home confused, but renewed, clutching the little red paper as though it contained movie magic and would rise out of my hand and unfurl to reveal the name of the husband I would acquire after the age of 35. In my room, I wrote a letter to the man on my mind. I said, *I went to see a Chinese fortune teller who told me to avoid bridges and sushi. He had golden eyes and piss-stained pants.* I paused to open the small red paper. Unfolded, I saw that, like the sign, the paper was written in a faded black marker. It was a mash of circular scrawls punctuated by a few dots. It was not Chinese. It was not hieroglyphs nor runes. It was not English nor artful nor otherwise knowable. It was a dried out marker pressed without prophecy into a scrap of red paper. I couldn't hold the illusion but I kept the paper for years.

Alice Through the Crowd

Can anybody tell me the time? An older lady comes shrieking through the mall. Brown floors, an IGA, an Aldo, a pretty low class place to spend a week's worth.

What's the time? Anybody please! Long nose, long grey hair, she was never beautiful. Her pink shirt is oversized and stretched out, she'd be pitiable if she wasn't repulsive.

4PM. The anonymous answer comes from a crowd near the food court.

4PM! OH GOOD GOD, oh god. I'm late!

The buzz on her heels on her exit is about

where could she be going and crazy old nobody.

The men are sniggering, the young women are snickering, the aging women are containing pity and repulsion and nodding their heads, tsk, tsk, tsk.

Flying down the escalator,

MOVE IT MOVE IT

The kids at the mall shoved aside for who is this shrew? what's with the witch?

It's summer and her slip-on comes off.

Oh NO, she shouts and tries to get it back.

Her shoe is buried between legs on the escalator and she pushes at them a bit trying to get up; the people are in a little panic.

What is she doing, excuse me lady, these things go down, not up.

All of them mad, it is almost literally, a SEA of angry faces, high and low grumbles.

EXCUSE ME I'VE LOST MY SHOE EXCUSE ME

What a crazy person, one man says

and upon retrieving the loafer our antihero clocks him upside the head and tells him,

MIND YOUR MANNERS

Wildly despised all over the Central Grove Shopping Center on a Saturday afternoon, Alice can not stop. She is racing through the mini-plex, sending shock-waves through the crowds of dissociated shoppers.

What a bitch, Jesus, what's the hurry, where's the fire?

Until Alice reaches the metro station at the bottom of four floors. Alice stops running, the metro hasn't arrived, she can tell from the screen that there are four minutes until the next metro. She sits on the bench, legs stretched, and lets one her shoes fall off, she lets her body sink into the tiled seat, she lets her eyes close. Wave after wave of shopped-out folk pass Alice to board the metro, remembering her, and the hurry she was in.

the Door on Your Way Out

Winter wasn't wicked this year. The year before last though, Nana came home and said, "What have you done?" She said, "Where have I gone?" We lolled around. We stood and wondered: why had Nana come back? She hadn't been gone long but it wasn't cheap to bury her in the first place. The whole affair was fine, a Paperman's. Party sandwiches and smoked salmon. We still wore the clothes. Our backs were sore from sitting in stiff chairs. "Get outta here!" my mother hollered.

"Get outta here, who needs ya!" I shouted after—also, as well, adjunctively. I threw in my two scents. It was weird, when I said that. It wasn't the right tone, the right time to add emphasis. But they quickly forgot as Nana sat down and started coughing. Mother got her a glass of water. Mother said, "Tell us about it."

Nana said, "What is there to tell?"

I sighed angrily and after weathering their testy faces I considered leaving the room. Every move I made was the wrong move. But I couldn't leave, not only would that also be the wrong move, but I wanted to know too.

"Well, where have you been?" I asked Nana—adjunct.

"In the ground—what?" she whined and complained that her water was warm. Mother brought her two ice cubes using her bare hands.

"I didn't see you wash those hands, but I'll have to assume that you did,"

Nana said. We watched her drink her water and heard her teeth clink against the cubes. She wasn't being useful. If she knew anything, it didn't seem like she was going to tell us.

"How long can you stay?" I asked.

"Stay," Nana said, "I just came for the water. I was thirsty, nu."

"Okay Mama," my mother said, "Well, I want you to know that we love you very much."

"Of course you love me," Nana said, "It's easy to love me now," she laughed to herself rather meanly. I had the thought that she might as well go if she was going to be like that and the moment I thought it she looked at me crossly.

"What?" I said. She looked harder and the black pits where her eyes should have been made a sound like a cicada. I'm sure that the ghost of my grandmother cursed me that day as I haven't had a date since the winter before last. But how could I help myself?

So, though winter wasn't wicked this year, it was lonely all the same.

Be Fruitful

"Rogerson's."

"Hi, I'd like info about your sign on 6th Avenue."

"6th and?"

"13th Street."

"What kind of info?"

"Information."

"In what sense?"

"I'd like to know what the sign is doing."

"What it's doing? Are you interested in buying space? Or is this more of a complaint?"

"Neither, it's a query."

"Okay I'll put you through to sales."

"13th Street sales?"

"Just the general sales department."

"Then why did you ask where the sign was?"

CLICK

"Jim here."

"Hi, I was wondering about your billboard at 6th and 13th."

"Just a minute here, let me take a look."

"Hi Ma'am, that space is rented. Did you have a business you were looking to advertise for?"

"No. Can you tell me who rented that sign?"

"What is this regarding?"

"I want to know what the big idea is."

"Is this a complaint, I can put you through to—"

"No, it's a query."

"Well, maybe I can help."

"I was hoping."

"What is your concern with the sign?"

"Can you tell me why there is a rotten pomegranate on the billboard at 6th and 13th? Who pays to have that there? What is the message?"

"I'm not sure I see the problem. . ."

"No problem, query."

"Oh, you want to know who paid for the pomegranate?"

"The rotten pomegranate, yes."

"Well, I have him down here as Dave."

"Dave?"

"Yes."

"But you don't know what he's selling or why he posted the pomegranate?"

"The rotten pomegranate?"

"Yes."

"No."

"Can I speak with Dave?"

"You want his number?"

"Yes."

"I'm afraid I can't do that."

"Okay. Well, can you pass along a message?"

"What's the message?"

"Hi Dave, I noticed you posted a rotten pomegranate in a field of yellowed grass at 6th and 13th. I noticed it at night, as it's being lit up at night. Did you know, Dave, that people can see the pomegranate even at night? I wondered if you could get back to me about this because I was startled to see it and I wasn't sure what barren message was being pasted or if it was intended it to be taken as such. As well, Dave, are you aware that there is an ad for chili on the other side of the billboard—"

"That's a different ad."

"I assumed."

"So why mention it?"

"I thought he should know."

"You think he doesn't?"

"Anyway, can you pass this message along? And have him take my phone number."

"Alright, but I can't say if he'll get back to you. We haven't spoken with him for some time. And, well, I shouldn't be mentioning this but, he paid for a seven year lease on the sign."

"Is this information confidential?"

"Seems like it ought to be."

"I'm not so sure."

"Okay Ma'am, well I'll see about the sign."

CLICK

"Oh, but—Oh."

Better you don't

Not right now but later I'll tell you about Diana, or Julie. Diana first. Diana wanted a baby. She was 30 years old and she had no partner and—I'm too tired for this. I need coffee. Diana Diana Bo-Bana Fe Fi Fo-Fana, she was desperate. She pricked pinholes in condoms, she buried plastic dolls in the garden like a spell, a witch's spell. She wrote to a woman online about her fears and her spells and the woman told her she was too weak to be feared, that she needn't worry about any damage her pathetic spells would do because she had barely the power to cast them. And Diana thought, *if i don't have the power, who could have the power, no one, no one has more need than i do, more longing, more desire, my*, she thought, *my fat wet heart is breaking*. She looked at artificial insemination but found it shameful, horrible; she couldn't say why. She just imagined the lie; she couldn't say that she couldn't find someone who would love her enough to want to make more of her so she would have to lie and pretend she wanted it this way and then she would have to lie to the child, and so the child would never know her, and the child would be tormented by his own fatherlessness and by his mother's pridelessness—she wouldn't do it. She thought about adoption, but it meant nothing to her; it had to be a piece of her, that's what she wanted, new flesh in the world, touring and living in youth with the knowledge that escaped her— to be more than she was, to be more than the entire last generation and yet imbued with their knowledge and the energy from youth to take it further. She couldn't adopt. She couldn't lie, and she couldn't be honest. She wrote back to the woman who practiced witchcraft on the internet under the name WindWoman and said *perhaps i am weak, if i can't admit what i desire, if i find shame in science and force myself to lie, perhaps i am weak, but how do i become strong, what is the next step* and the WindWoman said, "Stop grovelling." And Julie, she had several children with her husband Michael.

"Technically, it's a chanukkiyah" – Erica Strange

The Diaspora Jew is doomed to assimilation, by gentiles or by Israelis.
– Irving Layton, *The Whole Bloody Bird*

Some barely there relationship. Like I sent my mother a picture of these shoes I found with little menorahs embroidered on them. I didn't caption the picture—I don't know why, I usually would. People have to be told why I think something is relevant to our relationship or to the world or to whatever—but I didn't caption the picture and she didn't respond and it made me think there was like a little question, something in the air, maybe not, maybe she's taking her time, but it made me think—and the thought was about us: her relationship to her culture and then to mine, and mine to mine. I always felt like she wanted to be the person doling it out. Like I shouldn't want more Jewishness than the amount allotted for me, because it's hers. It's only mine through her. And my mother is a bit funny about it. Maybe funny, but not like Cousin Rachel funny. Rachel who buys "Get Lit" Chanukah sweaters but never lights a candle, dreidel socks but she doesn't know the rules of the game, "Oy Vey" aprons for cooks who can't cook, but with no more knowledge of Yiddish than a native New Yorker. My mother doesn't go in for paraphernalia as a way for Jews in the diaspora to be Jews, she doesn't even go in for a diaspora. She's Canadian. And she believes in assimilation. She believes in Christmas like it's a patriotic duty. And then, she lights the menorah when she can—she taught me a basic prayer. She knows it's there, this gaudy Jew scratching at the door, but it shouldn't intrude. And when it starts to intrude, she finds it ugly, out of control, not Canadian, un-Canadian. And so the used shoes two sizes too big with little embroidered menorahs, I didn't buy them for what could I do with them, hang them on a wall but never wear them without sliding out, slipping around, plus cracking my skull on the outside walk, slick with ice—in fact, who can wear a Chanukah ballet flat during Chanukah at all? It's cold in Europe, it's cold in Canada, so maybe they travelled here from diasporas unadvertised, or Florida before off-shoring, or China, really, made for a particular demographic—or Israel—where they care—to lure us to a place where they must assimilate to us, where we don't wear boots for winter. And yet I don't believe in the fences around the rules that let you boil water from a machine you start before sundown and use for the next 24 hours. "The machine is boiling the water, not me. I'm clearly behind the fence, far behind the fence, can't even see the fence from my safe distance."—This is the long logic that lets us, lets my mother equally say, "I believe it in my heart." And with such sentiment and internal miming of devotion the practice becomes moot, then the tradition, then the culture. The tall wall or fence erected through the thought that I *am it* so I don't need to *do it*. And maybe some little guilt and questioning seep in, like, is it enough? And that's the thing that makes her possessive, the insecurity that it's hers with little practice, with self-erected fences and idiosyncratic reasoning, through a really vague heartily removed knowledge of the Torah. So why do you need those shoes, so why is she sending me these shoes, maybe she wonders, maybe she thinks, shoes Canadian Jews can only wear with festive logic in Israel? Would I trump her so severely to take up practice in Israel? Renounce the grounding assimilative feature of her practice of feeling and knowing but not really being a part of anything? And if I did, her question would be, as my question would be, as is the question of the secular, scoffing a little, disbeliever would be: how could you like—do you really believe in God, or do you just like the shoes?

"In the End, Man Will Probably Peel his Skin"

Ms. Paley stood up on a park bench and her worn grey socks fell and bunched around the holes of her shoes. She tried to climb onto the armrest but stumbled back and settled for standing on the seat. She said, "Who's the bum who leaves the Kleenex in the halls?" and people walked quickly past. She said, "The truth finds its own level and floats!" and several people stopped and gathered around her grey ankles. She told the people gathered that whether or not their lives were ruined by monkeys, snakes, and seething teenagers or cured by durable plastics, they would remain, rain or snow or wind-swept pavilion, diurnal. And the few who had gathered, vacated, unsettled. We, sitting across from her, having a picnic smoke and a cherry coke, took notice. We remembered forever.

Love Me

"Very interesting. Very, very interesting," Doctor Balbud said and rubbed his chin.

"What is? What's interesting?" Jerrel begged Balbud. Balbud looked at Jerrel again, examining him, inspecting his skin, his hair, the freckles on his nose. There was one freckle off-center on his forehead that Balbud spent some time on. Balbud nodded, he exclaimed, he mentioned that he might have to get another doctor but seemed reluctant to leave Jerrel, as though there was something he might miss. Jerrel wiggled atop the crunchy sheet that lined the examination table. Balbud kept his eyes on Jerrel, eye to eye, then eye to nose, eye to tit, eye to belly button, all the way down—Jerrel thought the doctor might pull his toes, one by one, lovingly, as a mother might. Jerrel thought the doctor might pat his skin as though it were soft and irresistible. But Balbud resisted. Balbud studied Jerrel and called out in a bellow that ended in a shrill cry, "Nurse!" The nurse, a thick woman with dyed orange hair and a mean brow approached lazily. "Nurse, take a look at Jerrel." The nurse looked at Jerrel and found him a man of about 35, gangly, boney, and pale. Jerrel looked back at the nurse. The nurse cocked her head. She looked at his hair, mousy brown, his forehead, flat, with some fading acne scars, she looked at his muddy grey eyes, his wide crooked nose, his nose hair, his ear hair, she became obsessed with his left lobe. Jerrel thought she was salivating.

He thought she might put the ear in her mouth, not as a gentle lover, but as a grabby baby. "Wow," the nurse said. They begged Jerrel to remain in the office in his underwear. The nurse began writing. Balbud was making phone calls. Jerrel thought he heard voices at the door.

"What is it? What are you writing?" Jerrel asked half-heartedly. The nurse insisted he lie down. Jerrel laid and waited. Another nurse began buzzing around. A second doctor emerged from a nearby supply closet. There was a man in a blue coverall poking Jerrel with a broom handle but that's when Jerrel closed his eyes and decided to stop asking questions. He felt himself lifted and he felt the temperate summer air soft against his bare skin. Someone had removed his shorts and his balls dangled between his legs, his cock bounced with the steps of the crowd. His legs, his arms, his flat white buttocks, his jutting shoulder blades, his long neck, the mound of greasy brown hair atop his lollipop head, all supported by many hands. Jerrel kept his eyes closed. He felt taken care of; a child brought in from the car, a child who'd fallen asleep at the movies. There was a trumpet, there was the flap of a flag. Jerrel felt the sun against his eyelids, against his belly, against his toes. He heard a woman say, "The man is remarkable." He heard a child scream. He was being carried and Jerrel wasn't sure about the destination. He was being taken somewhere, maybe towards the sun, certainly far from the clinic now. He couldn't clearly remember why he had gone in the first place. He hadn't felt ill, not really. There was an all-around-ness that had been plaguing him increasingly for 15, 16, 17, 18 years or more and it seemed, he thought, about time to get it looked after. It was a general malaise, nothing too bad. There wasn't any cause, any trouble. He just went in, took off his clothes, sat before Balbud and waited. And Balbud alerted the press. They were there, Jerrel heard them.

"This is Channel Six."

"This is WMWV."

"We're on the scene."

"We're here reporting."

"Now, this is something we're sure you'll want to hear!"

Balbud might have been leading the parade. Or maybe, having discovered Jerrel, Balbud was off to the side, answering questions and signing autographs. Jerrel kept his eyes closed. He could feel everything anyway. He had seen everything anyway. After 35 years, he had a pretty good idea of what everything looked like and though he liked looking at it, it sometimes gave him a twitch of pain, a pang of despair; he didn't know why. It had something to do with the with-ness of it or the it-ness of it. It was there, he was here. There it was, beautiful, strange, menacing, everywhere, and here he was, thinking about it, appreciating it, cursing the wind, loving the bird in the forest, hating the bird on his window sill. He didn't need to see it. He didn't need to see anything. He felt all right. He felt like he had everything; this was everything he'd ever wanted. He had to keep it with him by keeping his eyes closed and the people loved him better with his eyes closed anyway—he didn't know for sure, but he suspected and he thought it was about time he started believing in suspicion. He also suspected that he had been waiting for this, that he had always wanted it and had been waiting for this moment of being seen and being known utterly and completely, embraced by sun and crowd with his balls to the sky. This was it, he had arrived. He only hoped, he only prayed, that the crowd would devour him before they dropped him.

Little Wisdom II

Miranda was afraid of being maimed. Was it the papercut or the paronychia that caused her hand to swell and hurt around the right-handed ring finger? She was guarding it, babying it, taking extra care of it, thinking anxiously while she half-slept that should she sleep wrong and cut off the circulation to the right side of her body the blood would be trapped, the finger engorged, and the infection would become further infected with some necrotic ever-expanding fester. She would have to have the hand removed and then relearn how to type and so relearn how to think. Waking after stressfully sleeping she stood up, put potatoes in the oven, made tea, and sat down. Everything took longer with extra care and she even found that the extra care for her infected hand left other parts of her uncared for—then burnt, on the rack of the oven, while removing an overbaked potato, her left hand. Worrying that the blister would be prone to infection unless she took care, she took *extra* care so she didn't lose both hands from un-regarded infections and so lose the typing that lets her think, lets her thoughts lay out in a line and not swim chaotically like lost members of little schools of fish shouting and smashing into to each other never knowing where they are going, where they are from, and to what relationship they have with the fish around them, and so eat the wrong fish, and so wrestle the wrong fish, and find, ultimately, no relief. Then while over-caring for her hands she found she used utensils much worse and cut her food very awkwardly and the overbaked skin of the overbaked potato was cut into chunks too large for her small mouth now working in weird ways and biting cheeks and tongue and causing blood to drip out onto the table and thus she became concerned that the hands are prone to infection and the mouth is prone to infection—though mouths heal quickly and she's less attached to mouths because the jumble of squished fish that swim from the mouth are better pushed back and upwards into the crowded pool of fighting mouth and gill breathers and then left to wait until a healed hand or proficient stump pulls them down and types a place alongside another, alongside another, alongside another, and you can see some sense in them then—but still, it might be hard to negotiate the hospital with no health card and no mouth and thinking this while taking a cloth and dropping the cloth on the blood and scooping the potatoes away into the sink, she uses her foot on the low table to sop up the blood to avoid using her hands and falls backwards and bangs her head against the lacquered concrete floor. She lays and wonders why she doesn't have carpet but remembers then the dust in carpet and the dirt in dust and finds concrete so easy to clean if not nearly deadly to fall backwards upon when wiping up the mess of the potato bloodbath with her foot to save her hands and protect her brain from rerouting information to who knows where, not her mouth if she's mouthless, maybe out her ears though in wax and fish and dripping things, and lying there thinking of the future of words crippled by hands, feels drowsy, and naps.

Ladies and Gentlemen

"A state of grace," Leonard Cohen said in response to an interviewer insisting, demanding, that he make an opinion. To wake up in a state of grace and return to bed if one wakes up without. Irving Layton, like a sigh, like "obviously" like "come on come on what my friend here really means" decides that the poet must protect himself, his psyche, the purity of his impression, from steamroller-ing. Cohen, without having become fashionable or unfashionable in sentiment, or relevant or irrelevant in content, nails it, explains to his pet interviewer that those who confront him, casually but nonetheless, are looking for the low-down, that he might reveal the con, and Cohen, almost wishing he had one, can hardly answer without a secret smile and a wink at the audience—the poet, the con, who plays himself.

Mrs. Yablunsky

I sat between Mrs. Yablunsky and Mr. Marchand at my Aunt Louise's house over Passover before the rift between Aunt Louise and Aunt Myrna. Ben and Myrna and their kids and Myrna's mother Mrs. Yablunsky stopped coming or being invited for the high holidays, though Mr. Marchand still came, and I still sat next to him as he was an uncle or something from Louise's daughter-in-law's side of the family. Before the rift—which I think was about somebody not getting a proper greeting on a night out at Moishes, or it might have been something about Louise not sending her regards to Myrna's granddaughter after the girl broke her collarbone—the dinners were large. Fifteen people or more sitting around a long table with several panels and no room to get out once you were in without shuffling and having everyone pull in their chairs and suck in their bellies.

Mrs. Yablunsky sat with tissue paper arms limp at her side as Louise piled on the brisket and handed it to me to hand down the line. Louise called on me to eat and take more and I did and passed it down to Mr. Marchand who nodded his head and met my eyes with his, clear and quivering blue. "*Merci*," he said, and I felt the plate drop a little when he took it. Louise loaded Mrs. Yablunsky's plate with meatballs and she sat impressively rigid with an approving but tight-lipped expression. "Which is your favourite?" I asked her.

"*Hein?*"

"Which dish is your favourite?"

"Oh," she said, trilling air from her thin lips. "I used to like Louise's meatballs, but I can't taste them anymore."

"Oh?"

"I can't taste anything. I think it happened on my 80th birthday." She laughed lightly like she had an inside joke not with me.

"It's lousy," she said.

"Yeah, it sounds lousy."

"It's LOUSY!" she said again.

"The brisket—"

"What's the point?" she interrupted, "I don't need to eat. I only leave the house when Myrna picks me up!"

"What Ma?" Myrna yelled from the end of the table, "Ma?"

Mrs. Yablunsky shook her head and waved her hand dismissively towards her daughter.

"I like staying home," I told her, " and watching TV."

"The TV, I always have on. Before Nachum was dead, we didn't have a TV. We played cards."

"Which games?"

She picked up her fork with one hand and the other hung down past the seat of the chair. She slowly flattened a meatball. "I can't remember. I can't remember a damn thing!" She laughed. I laughed too, and ate and thought about why Louise serves so much meat, why she serves chicken, meatballs, brisket, and fish. There's challah and knishes but nothing holding it all together—no rice, no mashed potatoes. It started with matzo balls, though Mrs. Yablunsky didn't take any, Mr. Marchand and I agreed it was our favourite soup.

Mrs. Yablunsky waved a fork with her right hand and called across the table to Louise's granddaughter Nicole, "Aren't you pretty!" The blond toddler eyed her suspiciously, whispered to her father, and slid off the seat. She pressed herself between the backs of the mahogany chairs

142

and the maple hutch, then danced towards her mother and grabbed a bald Barbie held by her little sister. Her father Barry watched with frozen interest and called to his wife, "Cybil, get the doll from Nicole!" and then to Nicole, "Give it back! Nicole, give it back!" And shovelled heaps of fatty brisket into his maw. Mrs. Yablunsky and I watched, and I willed him to make eye contact. Uncle Barry—I used to think he was so *cool*. He travelled the world in olive-green short shorts and hiking boots; he had a wiry beard, laughed good-naturedly over everything, and always took the left side. Four years and fifty pounds into family life, and he sneers out of the side of his food-full mouth over anti-austerity. Family dinners during my university years felt different. My Uncle Barry, who I guess is more of a cousin, but I had called uncle as a child; my mother's brother, Marc; and my cousin Heather's husband David would talk politics and morality and ethics and the recession and the student strikes. And now Barry slurps his meat, Marc died of cancer, David's at the far end of the table—probably the same as ever—and I'm more comfortable amongst the silence and slowness of Mrs. Yablunsky and Mr. Marchand who eats tidily, wore a beautiful blue suit, and combed his hair so neatly I could see bits of soft pink scalp between the combed partitions. "*Chère*, I like best the brisket too," he whispered to me as Louise began to clear the plates and Mrs. Yablunsky's mounds of half-mashed meat jiggled and slid. "Yes." I told him and we smiled and he patted my hand and I could have wept but for the Zoloft.

But Barry didn't look up, and Mrs. Yablunsky loudly sipped some water.

"I don't think he tastes it either," I whispered to Mrs. Yablunsky, with a side eye on Barry looking into his plate.

"*Hein?*" she shouted, crunched up her face, and looked at me like we'd just met.

Question on the Absent Concept Integral to Identity; or, The Rise of the NBC Homunculus

Lenny Cantrow died around 1989. It's approximate because he just sort of dissolved. Angelyne said that "when you die, you drop your total DNA into the world and everyone gets a piece of it." And that's exactly what happened to Lenny Cantrow. Do you remember him? He came into his own in the mid-1800s in the shtetl when everyone spoke Yiddish. Now only the old and the religious speak it. Maybe a couple of college students. You know by the time Lenny started getting attention in America he had lost all but the cutest Yiddish words, plotz and putz, tuches, and bupkis. He used them in his act, that great act that got him so many laughs in the Catskills, the one where he killed himself, dragged himself out, cuckolded himself and chased blondes, joked about his failure on the stock market, his failure as a man, a lover, a husband, a father, a friend, a Jew. It was spun gold. Maybe that's why it caught fire. Everyone was doing it; Cantrow was everywhere. Nebbish on the town. In 1978 *Time* said that 80% of comedy was Cantrow comedy. No one could get enough of him. Crazy to think that everyone knew his jokes but no one knew really his name. Part of the bit I guess. Even that grizzled Montreal detective knew it, the guy always telling it like it was, you know; and that slow moving poet, the one who was born old, he knew it too. Lenny failed even when he'd succeed, he'd moan and shrug for our amusement. He became known, overknown, dispersed, then only available for telethons, talking head and guest spots. People used the outline of him, he even became a *Simpsons* character. So by that time he was already satire. Post skewered, he hardly held a shape; a revised *Simpsons* character, something the writers adjusted well after the family went to Hullabalooza. He's psychobilly: adulterated. He's rustic sign night at the Cat Café. But what can you do when you're the ghost of an artifact besides join a historical society and spin Lil' Dicky records on a phonograph?

to whom life happens

On a page for synched media streams, in the dark mode, grayscale, 50 or more channels are listed in order of viewers; follows, the top three and the bottom two:

RealLYFERoom,Deal With It Assholes,Documentaries 24&7; Do Communists Have Better Sex? (Documentary); Connected 108.

🎬)) Movie Boi ((🎬 - top flicks 24/7/365 (movie_boi); tt0085811_Dracula_1992.mp4; Connected 65.

X ?? Seinfeld ?? X [html5] (no userscript); Season.08.Episode.19; Connected: 24

∞ ⚡ Harry Potter ❾¾ (Atmosphere); Harry Potter and the Philosopher's Stone.mkv; Connected: 4.

卐 ÜBERMENSCH 卐 - The National Socialist German Workers' Party; Sex, Productivity, and Motivation - ROBERT SEPEHR; Connected: 4.

A slow consistent chat runs alongside the videos in each channel:

human_soup:

ANOTHER POINT FOR MILOSH

[02:03:40]

rokosbish:

why is seinfeld so comfy bros

[02:13:12]

human_soup:

cos we're jewz

[02:46:04]

Notes

handwringers
In the essay "Funny, You Don't Look Jewish: Visual Stereotypes and the Making of Modern Jewish Identity," Susan A. Glenn notes that, in 1946, a "good deal of hand-wringing ensued" over a study that seemed to demonstrate that people who held strong prejudices against "Jews, blacks, and Catholics" also "tended to be the most accurate in their selection of Jewish faces." Glenn then notes that the "Jewish judges [Jewish people chosen to attempt to identify Jewish faces in pictures] proved to be what one study called 'unexpectedly incompetent' in identifying Jewish faces; however, in others [experiments] they demonstrated extreme tendency to see Jewish faces." *handwringers* is named with the Glenn text in mind.

Table of Contents (and more generally)
The inconsistent style of my titles has been mentioned and questioned—and yet I feel attached to particular arrangements of upper/lower -case letters, as well as occasionally idiosyncratic grammar and punctuation, on an almost emotional level and thus find it difficult to always (want to) stay within publishing standards when it feels as though an uppercase T or G or I changes some impression the story makes. While this is probably needlessly picky and neurotic of me, I think that there is some reality to these impressions. Consider what linguists call Computer-Mediated Communication (CMC), which refers to technologically mediated communication as a whole. Within CMC there are a number of micro-linguistic features such as emoji, eccentric spelling, creative punctuation, and the odd use of upper and lower case letters, to name a few, which are thought to arise in response to the lack of context clues inherent to technologically mediated communication. I am not a linguist, though I almost minored in it once; however, I do think that irregardless of how one feels about micro-linguistic features, they

operate in order to create additional meaning that may not necessarily contribute to any particular narrative but work to give words *life*, so to speak. Maybe a book isn't the place for CMC features, though I would argue that technological change alters our relationship to the whole and not just the part in which the change has originated (maybe that's obvious? Seems obvious). So while we may have developed grammar rules as a way of explaining what was already in use, we enforce those rules in order to give our work what? Consistency? Orderliness? The sense that we are doing the right thing when we do the ordered thing? Or so that our work may be judged alongside other work with some sense of fairness? Or so we can, in an official sense, all work towards some standard of knowing and understanding? I don't know. Lots of reasons. And I *like* knowing about grammar, punctuation, rhetoric, and editorial expectations, and I think the history of these things is worthy and worthwhile, but I don't want to get bossed around by them. Or as rhetorician Arthur Quinn put it: "The danger in a classification system such as this is that, like the robot which turns upon and begins to dictate to its maker, it can become an end in itself."

Skinning the Cat
Genesis 18:12: "And Sarah laughed to herself, saying, 'Now that I am withered, am I to have enjoyment—with my husband so old?'"

Colour Can't See
For a more in-depth conversation on Jews and race, see *The Jew's Body* by Sander Gilman.

Find the Bottom
This story is an adaptation of a tale told by Esther Bergner-Kish in the book *Folktales of the Jews: Volume 2, Tales from Eastern Europe* which speaks to the Yiddish proverb *Erger vi shlekht nit zahn* (It cannot be worse than woeful).

A Vote for the Vulgar Nightclub Clown
This story is in conversation with Philip Roth's *Portnoy's Complaint*: "Doctor, please, I can't live any more in a world given its meaning and dimension by some vulgar nightclub clown. By some black humorist!"

parts of the werld
Inspired by the Daniil Kharms' story, "THE WERLD," as well as an account of a scrap machine which Kharms apparently kept in his house in Leningrad in the 1920s.

Disgrace as their Portion
Proverbs 3:35: "The wise shall obtain honor, but dullards get disgrace as their portion."

Eulogy for the Man with the Trumpet
I've woven aspects of the life and work of Sherwood Anderson into this story—he was a strange, exceptional man whom I admire. For a thoroughgoing account of his life, see Walter B. Rideout's incredibly detailed *Sherwood Anderson: Writer in America*.

a timeless shrug
The title was taken from Ted Soloratoff's perceptive and erudite 1988 *New York Times* article, "American-Jewish Writers: On Edge Once More." The article is of a type of article that notes an interplay between success, acculturation, spiritual loss, and performative *schtick* for much of the American-Jewish diaspora, while tensions between modernity and tradition persist in observant communities, and the instability of Israel echoes, distortedly, that of exile: "Since the Palestinian uprising and the government's response, Israel has moved even closer as a subject; it looms now not only as the hero of our illusions but as the victim of its own; the face that shone its light upon us now bears a grimace, a scowl, a timeless shrug."

Heart to Heart
This story is an adaptation of a tale told by Gershon Weissman in the book *Folktales of the Jews: Volume 2, Tales from Eastern Europe*. Weissman's telling operates as something of an illustration of Proverbs 27:19: "A face answers to a face in water, so does one man's heart to another."

"Technically, it's a chanukkiyah" —Erica Strange
There's an odd moment in the largely secular 2010s CBC comedy *Being Erica* in which Erica Strange, while at a Christmas party, corrects someone's use of the word menorah. I had never heard the word "chanukkiyah" prior to seeing this episode and had always referred to the Chanukah candle holder as a menorah, as I will probably continue to do.

"In the End, Man Will Probably Peel his Skin"
The Little Disturbances of Man, Grace Paley

Ladies and Gentlemen
Ladies and Gentlemen... Mr. Leonard Cohen. Directed by Donald Brittain & Don Owen, 1965, for the NFB.

Sarah Mintz grew up in Greenwood, Goose Bay, Victoria, Courtenay, Vancouver, Montreal, and maybe even Moose Jaw — depending on how one defines "grew up." She's worked at video stores, thrift stores, pet stores, managed buildings, shoveled snow, and answered the phone. As a recent graduate of the English M.A program at the University of Regina, her work has thus far appeared in *Agnes and True*, the University of Regina's *[space]* journal, the Book*hug Anthology, *Write Across Canada*, and a chapbook, *The Zombie Stance of the Technological Idiot*, published by JackPine Press. Sarah lives in Victoria, BC.